WE WERE THE LANAKTALLAN OF THE ATOMIC HOOVES - A MEMOIR

Tales of the Terran Confederacy Book Four

Ralts Bloodthorne

Peeper Corner Publishing

CONTENTS

To everyone that has supported this amazing journey, I want to say thank you.

My wife, who is often bemused and startled at the living cartoon she married.

My kids, who made it to adulthood with a living cartoon for a parent.

My internet wife.

My friend Hambone.

And everyone on Reddit's HFY subreddit who supported and encouraged me.

All of you, thank you.

INTRODUCTION

Book Four of the Tales of the Terran Confederacy features the Lanaktallan "Ha'almo'or", a tank gunner who finds himself under-taking a job for more important.

This is sliced from the main body of First Contact and compiled here for ease of reading.

Enjoy.

PROLOGUE

During the waning days of the Unified Council, I was tasked with contributing to the defense of a small world. In the years gone by, I have largely forgotten the name the Council had labeled it with. I know it as Dulmara, as the natives renamed it.

History doubtfully shows little in regards to that battle. A protracted campaign that lasted, to me, forever that ranged across the entire megacontinent. I share with you the academic text:

The Siege of Dulmara was one extensive battle during the Second Precursor Wave during the Great Collapse. Terran and Unified Military Council forces banded together in the face of overwhelming odds to defend the civilian populace of 6.4 billion. At the end of the fighting, only 2.9 billion remained for the declared 'victory' where Unified Military Council and Terran Space Force military units authorized the use of atomic weaponry in atmosphere in reckless disregard for civilian life. This was not the first, nor the last time the Terran Confederacy used atomic weaponry in such a way as to put civilians in danger. The native species of Dulmara were left with a planet that had suffered massive ecological damage as well as a near total collapse of industry and agriculture.

That is it. That is all that appears in textbooks.

Those words, so easy for an academic to write, were not so easy when I was there.

I was but a lowly Tank Gunner Fifteenth Class, part of the Great Herd of A'armo'o, which was later renamed The Atomic Hooves. It was my first military deployment, and I had arrived with the tanks a fairly inexperienced gunner.

I gained my experience on the killing fields of Dulmara.

When we landed it was to reinforce the System Great Most High, who was concerned by the fact that the Terran Confederate Space Navy was operating nearby, establishing what was obviously a forward operation base to keep up operational tempo in Unified Council Territory.

We were barely there long enough for the tanks to be offloaded and readied for combat when the Precursors attacked.

I remember those days vividly. Some nights too vividly.

I can remember the rich smell of dropped patties when the internal waste system of the tank broke down on the second day, forcing us to scoop them out with chunks of plas and throw them from the hatches during our infrequent breaks. The smell of plasma round propellant, how it clung to my hide, to my armor, to the inside of my sinus cavity. The sweat, the urine, the flat taste of recycled water.

The fear.

The Precursors brushed aside the combined space fleets of the Unified Executor, Unified Corporate, and Unified Military forces like so much grain before a broom. They landed, in force, intent on stripping everything from the planet to fuel their unliving war machine.

Orbital strikes bloomed new suns on the surface of the planet, smashing down skyrakers like an angry child smashing a toy. Barely two thirds of the population reached the survival shelters.

The rest were on their own.

Out of General A'armo'o's twenty thousand tanks, less than half of us remained within days.

Half of the civilian population was dead with my comrades.

It was night when we heard the terrible news.

Terran Confederate Space Force was coming.

They announced themselves with **HEAVY METAL INCOMING** and I remember feeling despair. My tank was damaged from fighting the Precursors, most of the infantry was dead, and our air support had been swept from the sky like so many birds.

The bellow of **HEAVY METAL IS HERE** sounded like the death knell of the world.

Instead of attacking us the lemurs attacked the Precursors,

acting as if the Lanaktallan war machine was not even present. No vessel that did not attack them was attacked. Those foolish enough to attack were wiped from the skies.

Then we saw it. It looked like stars falling. Drop cradles carrying tanks. Drop pods full of infantry. Aerospace fighters sweeping into the atmosphere to bring the fight to the Precursors.

It was then I saw my first Terran.

More machine than lemur. Glowing red eyes. Large in stature and bulk. Cybernetics and adaptive camouflage. I have no words to describe the lemur commander. He was authority and competence made manifest.

I envied his men.

Our tanks were battered, damaged, beaten upon.

His were too, but it seemed almost as if it was the natural order of the universe that the lemur's tanks would be damaged.

I was shocked at how formal the lemurs were outside of combat.

I would learn, in the following weeks, that formality was a thin veneer over their savagery and fearsomeness in combat.

IN THE BEGINNING

I was born, possibly shocking enough, in the *Appreciation of Generosity Habitation Complex* on Hrrudra'antii-521, now named Shalluki System, on the 54th Level. I was my parent's fourth child, which meant their license and mandatory pairing was over. I was moved, by the time I was a year old, to the creche down on 64th Level. I was a mediocre student at best, with abysmal mathematics scores. I was uninterested in history, such as it was, but was able to focus on tasks well enough to slowly but surely ascend through the Unified School System. Upon my graduation, I took the tests, like any good Lanaktallan, and had a short list of less than twenty employment offers.

Being young, a merely 22, I had grown up seeing the Unity videos on the Tri-Vee. Visions of Lanaktallan all gazing upward at a future that was guarded by the Unified Military Forces. Handsome stallions in their sashes, vests, and flank coverings marching in unison down the street with their rifles. Armor covered soldiers guarding space ports and colonies.

Of course, the young me had no idea that those videos had been recorded tens of thousands of years ago. That the ideals I bought so whole-heartedly into were set down hundreds of thousands of years ago.

I signed up on the Level Five recruitment office. I was excited at the vast, dizzying array of jobs I was being offered by the Unified Military Recruitment System.

I can still remember trotting out of the Recruitment Center, a new sash proclaiming to everyone that I was a now a recruit, awaiting the next shuttle. I remember standing in the elevator, feeling proud of myself.

I would be a tank gunner. My reflexes, my eyesight acuity, my focus and concentrating offering me a job that had a wonderful signing bonus. Why, I even had a waiver for cost of training, lodging, food, and the pay of my trainers.

Two days before I was to board the vessel, a colt from Level 84 put an illegal needle pistol to the back of my head and had me transfer the balance of my account to his. Afterwards, he took my sash.

Still, two days later I found myself on a three month voyage to where I would receive my basic military training. I was broke, but wiser. My sash would not protect me, being part of the Unified Military Forces impressed nobody.

Little did I know, when I stepped onto the tarmac at the end of the flight, that I was on a collision course that would, less than three years later, have me shoulder to shoulder with enraged lemurs.

Eventually, beyond all reasonable predictions, I would find myself, wrapped in Terran warsteel and driven by Terran designed hover systems, wielding an atomic sledgehammer, in a place where even Death had died.

SCHOOLING

I arrived at the Basic Military Course on a warm afternoon, trotting down the corridor from where the shuttle had landed and into the concourse. I had my plas sheet with my Military Service Number emblazoned on it and I kept checking it against the signs that were scattered around. When I found the number I entered the room.

With nearly a hundred other Lanaktallan I waited to be told what to do next. Eventually a Tri-Vee came on, a robot delivered papers, and we were welcomed to one of the major Unified Military Forces armored vehicle training planets.

We were the next class, ten thousand strong, joining ten million already in training.

Training that, at first, was merely how to walk in lines, in synchronization, and how to appear to others. Chin up, upper shoulders back, arms folded, lower spine straight. Then to fire a rifle, how to wear armor, how to address one another, how to fill out paperwork, how to use a communication's device, how to give proper obeisance to our superiors.

In training I discovered that there were millions of my fellow trainees who had flunked out at various points, only instead of being sent home or to the mines they were just forced to start over again.

I also discovered that if you 'failed and recycled' all the costs were then waived.

Most of the hundred in my platoon 'failed' in the first few weeks in order to recycle and go through without accruing debt. As for myself, I had a waiver, so I just applied myself as I always had. Steadily working, being patiently, and not giving up.

Another discovery startled me. In the week after the final testing you could 'fail' for almost no reason, to be recycled. This was after class standing lists were put out, and awards gained during training were passed out.

I had achieved a certificate of Outstanding Achievement in the Field of Excellence of Parade Marching, which several of my peers had been motivated to be awarded. Those that wanted it, that didn't get it, dropped back and recycled.

I cared not. I wasn't a marcher.

I was a tanker, and tankers don't walk.

I graduated 2,388th out of 12,455. One of the few who had a guaranteed job after Basic Military Training. Because I was higher than 2,500 in standing I was asked if I wished to select a new Military Employment Field.

No. I wanted to be a tanker.

I was promoted, when I was sent to MEF School, and arrived with rank and awards on my sash.

My class was a hundred thousand strong, including the Lanaktallan who had recycled during MEFS. I was spoken to by the trainers. I had scored both low and high enough that I could choose to receive neo-sapient crew-member training. I considered it, pondering over it at lunch. My fellow trainees warned against it, that it could effect my future promotions and standings.

I took the training. Three months of learning how to be a gunner in a tank outfitted to allow neo-sapients to contribute to the might of the Unified Council. I graduated first out of the nine Lanaktallan who had chosen the training. I was promoted again, and offered 'Tank Crewmember Multi-Role Training', which would cover everything from Tank Commander to Gunner to Driver.

If I did so, I would forever give up the opportunity to be an officer, as no officer would stoop so low as to drive or fire the main gun.

Still, I liked the idea, so I took the option.

I was offered "Multi-Armored Vehicle Proficency School', again, I could not be an officer.

I took the offer.

Over the next year I learned, not only to fire the gun, but every other position in the tank and each type of tank.

During training, my ability as a gunner was brought out. I was the Trainee Host Champ and set a record when I hit 874 targets out of 1,200, setting a new record by over twenty hits.

Meanwhile, unbeknownst to me, a Terran tank crewman was somewhere learning to hit 800 out of 1,000, including while on the move. Terrans that my Star Nation had declared war upon with an unannounced attack upon non-belligerent worlds that were only peripherally aligned with the Terran Confederacy of Aligned Systems.

I was training to combat Corporate forces or break-away systems.

Terrans were training to kill anything that came into their gunsights.

I was in simulators.

They trained in real tanks.

I trained to fight on settled worlds, where I could leave the tank and breathe the air.

They trained as if the universe itself would kill them if they so much as peeked outside their tank.

When the news came that the Unified Council was at war with the Terran Confederacy I, like my fellow trainees, were confused at how the Terrans thought they could face the might of the Great Herd. Many of my fellow trainees were afraid the war would be over by the time out training was finished.

On the training world, things progressed as they had for millions of years. Something we had constantly drilled into us. Tank tactics had been finalized, streamlined, and made entirely efficient tens of millions ago. We were learning what the Great Herd had used to trample under all opposition.

I loved the tanks. Unstoppable engines of destruction, armed with plasma weapons to bring forth the fury of a star upon the foes of the Unified Council. Battlesteel armor capable of resisting any weapon brought to bear. Thick battlescreens that would prevent all but the heaviest weapons from reaching the heavily armored hull. Powerful hoverfans allowing the tanks to cross any terrain, even water.

Applying myself to training as I had everything else, with patience, attention to detail, and a hard work ethic, I was a first time complete on my travel through the training cycle.

The only first time through graduate in the entire Host. No other trainee had graduated after a single cycle of training in nearly three hundred thousand years.

Many of my peers mocked me. Told me that I was foolish not to remain in the cycles of training, to pass up chances for promotion based on how long I was in the Unified Military Forces, pass up the chance at awards, and the chance of making contacts with those higher ranking than me.

They didn't understand my desire to go somewhere and help defend the Great Herd.

Unlike my peers, when graduation came, and I was 525th out of 9,037, I accepted graduation instead of requesting that I be recycled.

And was assigned to Great Grand Most High A'armo'o's forces.

Little did I know that the simple random choice of units had slated me to become more than I had ever thought.

I was 25 years old when I landed, that sunny day, and pranced about excitedly at the thought of being assigned to my very own tank.

DISGRACE

A Great Herd Main Battle Tank Type XIX. IXTB-38A8r4. One hundred fifty tons of armor, molecular circuitry, guns, and hover-fans. Designed 638 thousand years ago and never having needed a single upgrade. A 180mm main gun that fires an eight pound plasma shell. Two rows of 80mm vertical launch systems capable of delivering a variety of variable fuzed munitions. A driver's, tank commander's, communications officer's, and an electronic warfare officer's external 18mm quad barreled plasma machinegun that could be controlled inside or manually by partially exiting the appropriate hatch. Capable of reaching a top speed of nearly forty miles an hour. The crew can survive inside the compartment for up to 11 hours without discomfort. Single layer medium grade battlescreens often used on light frigate naval vessels. Waterproof, soundproof, able to be piloted and operated even in vacuum thanks to sixteen antigravity pods, although at a much slower speed and slower response.

The mighty armored fist of the Unified Military Council, in support of the Unified Civilized Council.

According to my trainers, the last time a single tank had been damaged to the point that it could not fight, excluding operator error or sabotage, was nearly 23 thousand years prior to my introduction to my first tank.

I was excited as I inprocessed. I was to be assigned to one of the most modern tank designs around, military war machine made manifest. Perfection achieved and domination assured. I was almost eager the day I was allowed to enter the motorpool and taken to where the tank I would be a crew member of was parked.

It was love at first sight.

My fellow crewbeings thought I was a bit insane, to be honest. I worked on my tank, learning everything about it that I could from the neo-sapient mechanics. The driver was happy I could start it up for maintenance, meaning he could continue on with his long running alcohol related binge.

Within a month I could tear apart my gunner's sight, even the firing mechanism, and rebuild it from spare parts found in the motor pool supply shed. I even knew workarounds and field repairs that existed only in esoteric manuals and passed down in whispers between mechanics.

I earned my "gunner's bite" at my first live-fire range, where I learned that it was best if I let my helmet push back a little instead of pushing it against the padded sight. Pushing my face against the padding, using only my forward eyes, concentrating on putting each shot right where I wanted it.

Everyone took notice when I scored a perfect 1,200 points.

Some were happy for me, considered what I'd done proof of the Great Herd's might.

Others were jealous, starting whisper campaigns that I had somehow rigged my software to give me an illegal edge during live fire gunnery practice.

My fellow gunners led the campaign to have my accomplishment gone over with a fine toothed comb, many of them accusing me, to my face, of cheating.

My gunner's station was pulled apart, each block of circuitry examined, each byte of firmware and software gone over, even the gearing examined closely to see if I had somehow pulled off the shroud at the base of the barrel and adjusted the microgears that did the minute changes to barrel angle and elevation.

In the end, my score would have been stricken from the record, since my gunner's sight had gotten early maintenance, the neo-sapient maintenance crew replacing it twenty years before necessary. I would have been sent to do manual labor as punishment, or perhaps worse.

There was even talk of a court martial to put me in my place.

Mil-Sec officers had arrived in our motor pool to place me

under arrest when the sirens began to wail. Everyone looked around confused, even the Mil-Sec officers, at the tone of the siren.

It came over my implant at the same time as everyone's else, my lockout being lifted.

ATTACK IMMINENT -- PRECURSOR VESSELS IN SYSTEM IN FORCE

My platoon Most High began rearing up and down, screaming at all of us to get into ranks for inspection. The platoon Second Most High began galloping in circles, shrieking that we were all going to die.

He was wrong.

Only most of us were going to die.

TO WORK

The alert came across the datalinks on, first, the emergency broadcast channel. Then it was cancelled then broadcast across the General Command Frequency. That was cancelled and then the System Most High came over the Government Mandatory Announcement Channel on all of our datalinks.

I don't remember the exact words but he was panicking. I can remember, still, how he had foam around his jowls, how his feeding tendrils spasmed, how his eyes rolled in all six sockets. How his words were tumbling over one another and he babbled out over and over variations of 'we're all going to die.'

I was moving before my military police escorts, trotting away, toward the motor pool.

My tank was there. 15-281-31. My faithful tank.

I reached the motorpool when everyone else was still running in circles. I had stopped by the armory and found it empty, abandoned. I got my armor, which was to protect me from hull fragments spalled off by any hit that did not penetrate the armor but deformed the interior to spray shards of metal through the crew compartment. I had no personal weapons, a tanker I did not need them.

The motor pool was empty as I trotted through it.

I remember plas sheets blowing by in the winds. One stuck in my mind, a plas info-sheet informing everyone that possession of Terran media was considered subversive and would be punished harshly. It scraped across the plascrete, whispering.

It was then I heard it.

THERE IS ONLY ENOUGH FOR ONE

The shockwave hit me hard, but my armor possessed psychic shielding and I managed to keep my feet, staggering.

My tank waited. 150 tons of hovering death.

I went through the checklist, walking around outside of it. I activated and deployed the weapons. The tank had no ammunition, the weapons were disabled, but still, I deployed them and ran through function checks. When that was done I climbed in and went through each position, each station, activating them and running the proper preventive maintenance checks and services.

Once I needed to go get transmission fluid for the right forward number one nacelle fan gearbox.

Twice more I heard it.

THERE IS ONLY ENOUGH FOR ONE

The day was clear. Sunny, warm, a pleasant breeze.

I looked to the sky. Not for contemplation, but out of curiosity.

How long until the Precursors arrive?

Not long.

I returned to the motor pool master maintenance building, going through offices, until I found the keys to the munitions locker and the weapon locker.

I set about making my tank ready to fight.

When I had finished activating the weapons, arming them, loading the munitions bays, I sat beside the tank, waiting.

THERE IS ONLY ENOUGH FOR ONE

I shuddered, a trickle of blood oozing from my nostril.

My Company Commander galloped by, tearing at his own mane with his hands, ripping at his own face, screeching as he kicked and lunged down the road.

My helmet clinked and I activated the communications channels.

What I heard filled me with relief.

"This is Armored Host Most High A'armo'o. All troops, to your tanks. I am with you."

LEFT BEHIND

Even with Great Most High A'armo'o ordering the armories to be opened, the tanks to be brought up to fighting shape, and the crews to report to their tanks, it was nearly an hour before the crew of my tank arrived. The Planetary Civil Defense Network had ordered everyone into the shelters, and GalNet News channels showed lines of beings orderly moving into the shelters, which had been expanded in the last two years of the war to fit not only the Lanaktallan, but the neo-sapients and near-sapients.

The reality to that apparent care for those often deemed 'lesser' was less about their lives and more to prevent the Terrans from arming them to create instant reinforcements.

Finally, my crew arrived, seeing that I had prepared the tank, ensured the maintenance checks had been run. I had even loaded the ammunition bays and prepared the weapons for combat.

An argument started between the driver and the tank commander about whether or not I should be allowed to join the crew. The company commander had last been seen smashing his face against the side of a crashed ground car and the battalion commander called the two arguing sides idiotic fools, none of which stopped the argument. Ultimately they went to the Brigade Most High, who had advocated most strongly that I be jailed for my crime of scoring a perfect gunnery score.

The Brigade Most High had listened to the tank commander's reasonings why his crew should suffer having a criminal in their midst as well as the driver's impassioned pleas to remove my corrupting influence from the tank.

Three hours later I watched as the tanks I had trained among drove away, leaving me behind. Including 15-281-31. My faithful tank. It was going into battle with a gunner who had scored less than 12% hits during the last gunnery range.

Not knowing what else to do, I went into the maintenance crew break room. The neo-sapient mechanics were there, all watching with horror as the Precursor Autonomous War Machines first took over the broadcast waves and then broadcast their own feeds onto the channels in order to spread terror and hopelessness.

City after city was being blotted away by orbital strikes. Sometimes two or three strikes upon the same city.

I knew that the Precursors were attempting to destroy the shelters beneath the city.

The neo-sapient mechanics all gathered around me, unsure of what to do.

Finally one voiced the question: May I go be with my family?

I used a pry-bar to break open the metal box where the electronic keys for the minor vehicles were, passing keys out to those who could drive. I urged them to bring their families back, load them all into the trucks.

Those that stayed behind, I asked to assist me.

The munitions lockers were hardened structures, underground, climate controlled, designed to handle a near miss from a heavy atomic weapon. Reinforced to (hopefully) resist the weapons of the mad lemurs of the Confederacy.

We moved furniture we took from a nearby building, they watched in fear as I broke open vending machines and food dispensers. Twice I used the cable and hood of a tow-tank to tear a food dispensing unit clean out of the wall. We worked together, far into the night, to load the munitions bunker with food, water, rough furniture. I even had two mechanics install an atmospheric reclamation unit usually found in a heavy tank inside, just in case. I had two teams working feverishly to convert the dozen munitions bunkers that had formerly held plasma rounds and rockets into something that might protect them.

The neo-sapients urged me to come with them as I stood at the entryway and shut the heavy door that we had stenciled

"ALIVE INSIDE" upon, using Terran and Unified Standard Characters.

I shook my head and told them that my duty was the defense of this world.

They argued that I had no tank, I could not help defend the world.

I just smiled, and waved goodbye as the fifty-ton door shut and the locking mechanisms engaged.

When I trotted out it was raining a fine ash and I looked up at the night sky.

The clouds were burning.

I checked the load on my plasma rifle and my neural pistol, then checked my armor. I loaded up the maps and ran a search for what I was looking for.

Hab complexes.

I trotted over to the hovertruck I had used to commit theft of government property. I started it up, the number three fan motor screaming. Two neosapients and one near-sapient who had been hiding in the offices ran over and climbed on the truck, their faces obscured by their protective masks.

They would not let me carry out my mission alone.

Nodding, grateful for the company, I put the hovertruck in gear.

I turned it, oriented it, and drove.

Toward the burning city.

There were others there, I knew there were. The mechanics had told me of habs full of neosapients that had no where to go, that the hab complex itself had been labeled a shelter.

I had sworn to defend the Unified Council Systems.

And although I had no tank, I would not abandon my oaths.

The city was burning. It was a huge metropolis, and the unliving horrors from beyond the stars had targeted it repeatedly. We drove by those who had been caught out in the open by the kinetic blasts, their crumpled and often burnt bodies mute accusations that I had already failed in my duty.

We rushed for the first hab, using the massive weight of the armored recovery vehicle smashing aside rubble and wreckage alike.

THERE IS ONLY ENOUGH FOR ONE!

The roar of the Precursor Autonomous War Machines echoed through my mind. My fellow desperate crew members winced, but I had ordered them to install psychic inhibitors inside their helmets hours before.

I heard my fellow crew members weep, beg 'Overseers' to stop, to stay away, when they charged out of open doorways or alleys, rearing and screaming, their eyes bleeding, their ears and jowls often torn away.

I only had to order them to fire once.

Afterwards, they seized their courage and fired without the need for me to order them to.

A hoverbus lay abandoned and I ordered two of my men, and they were, looking back, indeed my men, to procure it and to follow me. It shuddered and was in need of maintenance, but it was public transportation for neo-sapients, which meant it was big enough that I could have loaded eight tanks, four end to end and two rows, into the bottom of its dual decks, and had room to spare.

We drove through the darkness, using the light amplification of our protective masks.

Flames flickered in the debris. Explosions continued further into the city. Ash rained down that tasted of scorched metal and burnt meat even through the filters of the masks. The sound of sentient suffering echoed off the buildings, a constant backdrop to everything.

We drove on, my crew and I.

Mal-Kar, a N'Kooran hoverfan mechanic, who, like me, could drive great unwieldy beasts. He had faith in me, for I had always treated him kindly and twice had defended him against accusations that he had purloined someone's lunch. He wore a modified tanker's helmet and spoke with quiet words.

Feelmeenta, a Hamaroosan electrical system specialist who had left behind her kits and little ones in the 'shelter' to hide in one of the offices to join me. I had ordered her into the shelter but she had laughed and told me that she was a near-sapient awaiting her people to send word for her to return, and that she would do as she wished. I knew better than to try to force her, Hamaroosa bit and pinched hard.

Julkrex, a Telkan gunny systems specialist, who had done the maintenance to my tank's gunner's sight, that I had not named when I had been rigorously interrogated. He had not returned to his people's homeworld, for reasons of his own, and I was glad to have him next to me as we drove into the burning city.

No better men existed than those who rode with me into that burning city, as no better men have existed than those you called brothers while fighting your own battles and wars.

Witness their names, readers, as you are witnessing mine.

We reached the nearest hab, using the recovery ball's gravitonic attachment system on the endosteel barrier over the entrance to yank it free. The neo-sapients within only saw armored and armed beings ordering them to board the hoverbus and did so meekly, as quick as they could.

I did not dispel their assumption we were ExecSec forces.

Twice I helped carry aquariums full of Leebawan tadpoles down to the bus.

It took nearly an hour to load the bus, an hour I felt often that we did not have as explosions rocked the city. Several times streaks of light connected the burning heavens to the hellscape ground and the shockwave rolled over us.

We headed back, the armored recovery vehicle in the lead, with our precious cargo of frightened and sobbing civilians.

I wished, more than once, I was inside my faithful tank, on the front line, protecting these people, these sentient beings like me, far more effectively than I could ever protect them driving a simple maintenance vehicle into the devastated city.

It started with only a few alerts. The vehicle was designed to recover disabled or damaged tanks from the front lines, and because of that, I was alerted whenever a tank was damaged or destroyed.

It started with a handful of alerts. Then more.

Then a steady cascade.

The Great Herd had millions of tanks on the planet.

But they were dying by the thousands.

I cursed my ancestors for creating such monstrous creations. My fellow tankers were all brave, as I was, skilled and capable. But they were facing an enemy that had no hesitation, that operated with the speed and precision of computerized mechanism. They would not error, would not hesitate, would not back down, and would not care for casualties among their unliving ranks.

I prayed, to whom I knew not, that my fellow members of the Great Herd would find their valor to not be lacking before the cruel precision of the Precursor Autonomous War Machines.

I remember Julkrex saying "A curse upon all engineers and programmers for what they have wrought upon us this night" and agreeing with all of my being.

The second crew had been hard at work while we had been recovering people from the hab, and they had completed work on the second and third munitions bunkers. We stood there, armed, armored, faceless behind our protective masks, holding weapons and watching the weeping neo-sapients enter the bunker.

I hardened my heart and soul as I stood and closed the door despite their weeping pleas to free them.

It was not yet midnight as we headed back into the city.

Just me, my faithful crewmen, our glorified tow-truck, and a hoverbus with armor hastily attached.

I had no tank. I was not manning any gun.

So I did only what I could.

Sometimes, in the dead of night, I ask myself...

was it enough?

BURNING

Slatmurt was burning. An entire planet was burning.

Dawn of the Second Day was a burning thing. The sun rose and shone its burning face upon a sky that was already consumed by fire. The clouds were bloody and bruised looking, the ash getting thicker as it rained down upon us.

We had filled five of the fourteen ammunition lockers with civilians, all of whom begged us to let them go, to free them, as terrified of us as they were of the Precursors. Their fear blinding them to the furniture, the food processors, the bedding, the recreational material, and the atmospheric generators. Blinding them to the fact that I was not imprisoning them behind a door that had the Terran words for "ALIVE INSIDE" written on the door under the glyphs of the Great Herd.

I hardened my heart as I closed the door on their weeping pleas.

As dawn arrived I gathered with my men, my loyal soldiers, in the armored fuel bay. I gave the orders for them to eat, drink, and try to rest.

The ground rumbled beneath our feet as the city took another kinetic kill hit from orbit.

We slept with our helmets on to spare our minds.

Even then, the nightmares were terrible. Full of pain, death, destruction, and torture. Always at the cold metal claws of the Precursors, who whispered in gleeful code bursts that there was only enough for one, and how I would not be that one.

It was nearly dark when we awoke, took care of biological imperatives, and left our little fortress.

The city was burning.

Great clouds of black smoke were climbing to the sky, the bottom of the clouds flickering and painted red by the fires consuming a city where only a day before millions of sentient beings went through their daily routine. As I watched a sky raker tilted slightly, then collapsed, the upper floors slamming onto the lower floors, compacting the building as it dropped.

Nearly three seconds after it began to fall we heard it start its death scream.

I wrung my four hands together with anxiety as I stared at the burning city. I could hear people screaming, a constant hellish wail that carried all the way to the military base. I could see the suburbs burning, see the great hab-complexes on fire or collapsing.

"I cannot order you to accompany me into such hell," I told them.

"You are our Most High, Ha'almo'or," Feelmeenta told me, wringing her hands on her prybar as she stared at the burning city. "Where you lead, we shall follow."

"We are the only ones who can do thus, so we must," Mal-Kar said softly, his eyes wide as a hab complex slowly began to collapse. My implant told me that we had cleared that one and I felt relief that we had done what we could. "No matter our fear, no matter how badly I want to go home, I will not leave them, or you, behind me when the current turns and threatens to become an undertow."

"The Digital Omnimessiah does not demand fearlessness, merely encourages mastering one's fear to do what must be done if a being is the only one who is capable of doing it," Julkrex told me, adjusting his helmet.

Most Lanaktallan would have been aghast at the mention of the Terran religious superstition. An Executor would have summarily executed him right on the spot.

But most Lanaktallan weren't staring at a city slowly being consumed.

"Then pray to your electronic deity for all our sake, Julkrex," I stated. I checked the charge in my plasma rifle. "We go back in."

My men put on their protective masks and we did preventive maintenance checks and services on our two battered vehicles. The armored heavy equipment recovery combat utility lifting extraction system vehicle, who's number two fan howled and vibrated and stunk inside of fear and desperation. The hoverbus, riding low with the addition of hastily welded armor, but able to carry hundreds at a time.

As I drove my upper torso and head were outside the armor, standing up in the driver's position, one hand resting on the dual barreled plasma machinegun, the other on my helmet, and my lower two hands steering. On the bus I could see Mal-Kar driving, the macroplas missing in front of him after a piece of debris had shattered it.

We followed out path into the city, the hoverfans roaring as it allowed us to traverse the heavily damaged streets.

We cleared two habs in twice as many hours, shutting them into the shelters despite their urgent pleas to free them, to not lock them away and imprison them.

It hurt, in some strange way, that they didn't understand I was trying to save them rather than ladle additional cruelty onto their lives. It hurt me that they did not trust me, not because of anything I had done before, but because of what my people had done to them.

Their small apartments, so bare of simple luxuries like colored paint on the walls, the cracked and crumbling plascrete of their housing, their food dispensers that were more restricted and bare bones than the ones I had used during military training. Many of them were eating unflavored nutripaste, the paste so thin it was like watery gruel, when we marched them from their apartments at gunpoint.

A part of me was ashamed, but I pushed that aside, and marched them down, out of their homes, and onto the bus at gunpoint.

I let them think I was an Executor or worse.

What they thought of me did not matter as long as I tried my best to save their lives.

My men knew why I was doing what I did. They understood, as they stood next to me, armed, faceless and featureless in their protective masks.

It was at the third hab of the night, just a handful of minutes before midnight, that we ran into opposition for the first time.

We came around the corner of the massive hab complex, which held two thousand families, only to see that there were four Executor vehicles blocking the street halfway down, with about three dozen armed and armored Executors guarding the primary access point of the hab while a handful of engineers welded a dur-alloy sheet over the door.

We slowed down and I moved my hand from where it rested on the plasma machinegun to the controller down inside the hull.

One Executor, red piping down his armor, held up one hand as he trotted toward us.

"What are you doing in the city?" he demanded more than asked.

"Rescue operations," I replied.

"I have no rescue operations listed for this area of operation," he said.

"I apologize for any misunderstanding. My orders were ver-bally delivered from my Most High," I lied. I had prepared my story in case of running afoul of any Sec Service the night prior.

The Executor officer stared at me through his clear face shield and I could see the lights on his datalink flashing.

He suddenly jerked, looking at me, and I knew, somehow, that his computer systems had managed to identify me as a known criminal with a harsh sentence.

"Shut down the vehicles and exit them with all due haste!" he ordered. Behind him his men charged their neural rifles and lev-eled them at us. "You are under arrest. You will comply and submit to us. We will take you into custody and you will be remanded to military justice authorities."

I looked past him, at the building, at all of the neo-sapients staring out their windows at what was going on. I knew they felt hopeless, felt bottomless despair, being welded into their habs as supposed 'shelter' from the Precursors.

We Lanaktallan were supposed to be the stewards of over two dozen neo-sapient races, near civilized species, and civilized species.

This was no stewardship, what the Executors were doing.

My thumb found the safety switch on the handle I was holding.

"Submit to my authority, lowly one," the Executor stated, his hand moving to charge his neural rifle.

"I am sorry, Executor, but there is a simple problem with your assumptions," I told him.

He frowned, confusion filling him as I made no move to shut down the armored beast nor to leave the vehicle.

"What problem?" he asked.

"A simple mistake in your logic chain," I told him.

He was unaware of what was happening off to the side of the recovery vehicle, focused entirely on me.

"What mistake?" he demanded.

My thumb hit the firing stud on the remote gunnery station and the dual barreled plasma machinegun roared, the barrels spinning to allow one to cool for a split second as the other one spit purplish-white darts of burning hot protomatter.

The Executor exploded into rags of tissue and Executor armor as I shifted the gun and raked the Executors gathered by the vehicles.

The other two guns on the recovery vehicle opened fire as Julkrex added his skills to the firefight.

Feelmeenta raked the ones at the door with her own rifle, set on the fast pulse setting.

Within seconds it was over. The Executor vehicles burning, adding their smoke to the haze of the murdered city. The dead were scattered around, none of them having gotten off a single shot as the situation changed too rapidly for them to process.

"Your mistaken belief I will come along quietly," I told the smoking half-corpse, my finger still keeping the barrels rotating to cool them down. I threw the recovery vehicle in gear, moving down the street.

The plenum chamber scraped the road, reducing the charred body of the Executor Most High into a smear on the pavement.

It took less time than usual to load up the hab inhabitants. We gathered up the weapons, storing them in the recovery vehicle.

It wouldn't do for a child to find them.

When we reached the motor pool I stared in shock.

A single tank had returned. Its armor was damaged, smoking, and two fans were out. The gun was warped, but it was a tank all the same.

I kept staring it as I urged the neo-sapients into one of the refurbished bunkers. The work crews were hard at work, having gotten all the way to the eighth and ninth bunker. Part of me noticed that the work crews were larger than they had been.

An aid station had been set up, manned by several Hamaroosa and a N'Kooran.

Once the refugees were safely into the modified munitions bunker I moved to the aid station.

There was a single Lanaktallan there. He was bleeding from his ears, four of his eyes had ruptured, and one of his jowls had been torn away, revealing his teeth. He had suffered burns on his lower body and as I trotted up the Hamaroosa tending to him shook her head silently.

I knelt down next to him. "What happened?" I asked him, taking his unburnt hand in mine.

I had learned the value of physical contact helping the neo-sapient refugees.

"Too many of them. Our guns are almost worthless," he gasped. He looked at me, but I knew he wasn't seeing me. "We tried, Most High, we tried to hold them back, but there was too many of them."

"It's all right, faithful one," I said, reaching out with one hand and touching his unburnt shoulder. "You did more than anyone should ask."

"We shot our guns dry. My crew, Most High," he began to

weep. "My crew, they all died. A rocket hit my tank, the crew compartment exploded," his weeping became stronger. "My gunner, he still got his shot off, Most High," I could hear the pride behind the tears. He looked at me, squeezing my hand tightly. "Tell my mother..."

He went limp. The fire left his eyes.

I turned and looked at the tank. It was from another Armored Host, one I did not recognize. It was not surprising that I did not recognize the tank.

Almost half of the Great Herd's armored units were destroyed. The infantry units were deserting, according to the communication chatter I had listened to in the armored recovery vehicle.

"Should we fix it?" Mal-Kar asked me. "If we use the robotic repair bay it's an hour's work at the most."

"Yes," I told him. "We'll need it."

"For?" Julkrex asked, as if the smiling Telkan didn't know the answer.

I turned and looked the way the brutally damaged tank and its dying commander had arrived from.

"They're coming."

FROM BAD TO WORSE

While Mal-Kar drove the tank into the robotic repair bay I approached the work crews busily clearing and upgrading the bunkers. They all clasped their hands together respectfully as I approached and I waved at them to go back to work, looking for the leader of each of the (now) four crews.

The leader of the first one, a Shavashan by the name of Tan'Kurik, went to set down his magnetic rivet gun and I waved at him to forgo the normal bowing and scraping.

People were dying. People. I had no time for such formalities that my people stressed even at the most dire times made me want to fire flared in the air and scream in rage.

"How may I serve, Most High?" Tan'Kurik asked.

"Go through your crews, find out who still has family in the city. I will not leave them to the mercy of the Precursor's claws," I told him.

He nodded and I moved away, going to each crew leader.

By the time the bus was unloaded I had a list of habs.

Three of them.

And a hospital.

I kicked myself for not considering the vast neo-sapient medical center just inside the city.

"Men, we have to go!" I shouted, running for the armored recovery vehicle. Mal-Kar ran to the bus and together we drove back into the smoke and flame of the city. I kept one hand on the control for the remote controlled 15mm plasma dual barreled rotary machinegun, the electronic eye of the weapon slaved to my protective mask's lenses.

The vehicle was not fast, it was built for power not speed, but the thick armor and the sheer bulk of the massive machine meant that the scattered burnt out vehicles were no impedance to our progress toward the hospital.

The hospital was intact and for that I thanked every being I could remember from Julkrex's prayers.

It took forever. Nearly three hours to clear out the hospital of the sick and injured.

The nurses and doctors that were still present objected to the fact I loaded them up in the armored vehicle until they saw that I had loaded them in with the most precious of our cargo.

The infants and children and pregnant beings, even the egg incubators.

Twice more we heard the scream from the skies.

THERE IS ONLY ENOUGH FOR ONE

The words made everyone flinch and I saw the power drain to the psychic inhibitors I had cranked up to over three quarters of the way to maximum. The large bus, in addition to armor, had been sporting installed dampeners and I was, as I had been many times over the last hellish hours, glad that I had ordered them installed.

I went slower than normal, allowing the massive machine's bulk to keep the vehicle steady, just a slight rocking motion.

It was long past midnight by the time we returned.

We escorted the newest ones to the ammunition locker that I had asked the refit crews to use every bit of medical equipment they could strip from the nearby military medical center, which had been abandoned the day before.

Mal-Kar was readying the bus when we saw the first of them.

Powered armor infantry.

The ran by, not stopping, heading from east to west, bypassing us as if we weren't there. Some had marks on their armor, but most of them had unblemished armor as they ran by at speeds you would need a hovercar to match. Most of them were without weapons and all of us stared at them as they ran by.

I knew what it meant, even if my men did not.

The lines were collapsing.

I moved over to our aid station, which, so far, had treated the dying tank commander and the injuries of the work crews. The N'Kooran came over at my bidding, ducking her head slightly.

"Treat any who need it. If they try to take the supplies, let them. Do not attempt to fight them if they rob you. They are panicked and will harm you, and you are more important than any medical supplies that I could scavenge from a treatment clinic," I told her.

She looked doubtful but nodded.

I went over to the tank, which sat, pristine and new looking, and climbed inside. I charged the powerplant and fired it up, the armored behemoth vibrating around me. Putting on a helmet I listened to the communications channels.

They were chaos.

Orders, counter-orders, panicking officers. Some called for retreat, others for an advance, still others called for digging in. There were requests for medivac, close air support, extraction, and the sound of panicked pilots refusing to enter the fray.

I switched to the tank command channels, wishing I knew which channel my own armored host was using.

The Most High of the Eighteenth Armored Host was screaming that they were all going to die, that they could not face the Precursors.

It was then I heard his voice.

"And where will you go, Du'unmo'ot? Will you sprout wings and fly away like an akltak hatchling? Perhaps you will launch yourself to moon on your own flatulence?" Most High A'armo'o asked, his voice calm and full of confidence. "Will you and your men die fleeing battle or will you stand and fight?"

"We cannot fight them! Our weapons barely damage them! They outnumber us! We can't hold them back!" the Sixteenth Most High bleated out.

"But our weapons do damage them," A'armo'o said. "Precision, speed, and application of your training and experience will carry the day."

I could hear the sound of a tank's plasma cannon firing behind Most High A'armo'o's words.

"The infantry has broken! We have no air support!" another Most High screeched. "All is lost!"

The tank suddenly chimed and my radio automatically switched channels.

"This is Most High A'armo'o, Great Most High of the Armored Host. Stand fast, do not flee the line! There is no place to run, no place to flee too. The Precursors are here and now is when your mettle shall be tested," the Great Most High said. "If your leaders have abandoned you, tie into the battlefield tactical network I am providing. If your subordinates have fled, tie into the network and I will assign you those who still possess the will to fight."

There was silence and I reached out one shaking finger, pressing the button to link the tank to the battlefield tactical network. The tank pinged several times and I was connected.

"State Identity."

"Gunner Ha'almo'or."

"Identity confirmed. State vehicle status," the VI said.

"Repaired and refit. Munitions fully loaded," I answered.

"State crew status."

"Gunner only."

"Confirm: Gunnery station only."

"Confirmed. Gunner only."

"State command structure status."

"None."

"Confirm: No command, local or otherwise."

"Confirmed."

It was silent for a moment and I wondered if I was to be abandoned again.

There was clicking and I was surprised at the voice I heard.

"Gunner Ha'almo'or, the network has you still in your motorpool but in a tank belonging to another Armored Host," Great Most High A'armo'o stated. "That tank was listed as destroyed fifteen hours ago."

"The commander managed to reach this location. He died during treatment. I had the tank repaired and reloaded. Fifteen of the forty bunkers are depleted, but I still have munitions and re-pair facilities," I told him. I waited a second and before he could reply I blurted out what I had been doing. How I had been pulling civilians from habs and the streets and the rubble.

He was silent a long moment.

"Gunner Ha'almo'or, I fear I must charge you with a grave task," Great Most High A'armo'o said.

"I do not fear, Great Most High," I told him.

"Continue your mission. What you are doing is far more than one more gunner. I know you are eager to engage in battle, but without saving the civilians, all of this is meaningless," his voice was serious and it felt as if he was standing next to me. "I will list your station as a refit and rearming point with medical support, but continue what you are doing."

"Save these people's families, Ha'almo'or. A'armo'o, out."

I sat in the tank, my chest full of something I could not iden-tify. A feeling of pressure, of pleasure, but also, in some way, of pain and anxiety.

I shut down the tank and left it.

I joined my men.

Together, we returned to the city.

The screams welcomed us.

More and more powered infantry ran by, some stumbling, all of them scrambling over what was in front of them, their minds so robbed by fear that they could not consider going around an obstacle, but could merely rear up and paw at it with their front hooves and beat on it with their armored fists.

Vehicles began speeding by. Light attack flitters. Most un-scarred, unmarred. All packed full of armored infantry.

All fleeing the front lines.

They ignored us, fleeing toward the west, toward the moun-tains, galloping through the city with no thought in their mind but running.

When dawn came we were exhausted.

Tanks waited to be reloaded and refit. Several neo-sapients manned the equipment, just overseeing the computerized robotic systems.

The tank I had talked to Great Most High A'armo'o was gone. I hoped, when I realized it was gone, that the new crew would be as dutiful as the commander had been.

I chewed stimcud, my men chewed stimgum, and we went back in as a bloody dawn rose.

It was almost noon when we heard it.

The only thing that could make things worse.

THERE IS ONLY ENOUGH FOR ONE roared out.

And for the first time, there was an answer.

HOLD THE LINE, BROTHERS! WE ARE COMING!

The Terrans.

The Terrans were coming.

AGAINST THE PRECURSORS

I was a mere Gunner Fifteenth Class when we heard the sound that any member of the Great Herd's military forces dreads to hear.

HOLD THE LINE, BROTHERS!

It roared out over every speaker, from every pane of glass, echoed from every flat surface, blinked from every pane of smart-glass and every display.

The call to arms of the Terran Confederacy.

The pre-battle warning roar of the universe's most terrible creation.

Insane highly intelligent bipedal lemur primates with enough savagery to fill a dozen other species.

I closed my eyes, all four of my knees shaking, my crests inflating protectively, as the sound roared out.

The Precursors were here, and that was bad enough.

But the Terrans?

That was like discovering that the fire you are battling is about to be stopped by detonating a nuclear weapon. Sure, it stops the fire, but at what cost?

My knees started to buckle as despair filled me. A black yawning maw full of eyes and tentacles that reached out for my soul to drag me into the depths and render me nothing more than a shivering bag of meat who's mind had shattered.

A Telkan female passed me, unseen, crying softly.

I heard her sounds of distress, the pitiable sobbing reaching through the darkness, through the horror, through the terror, a sound of anguish of a being who was powerless to do anything to save a life being destroyed all around her.

Strength filled my body, filled my soul, and I straightened up, opening my eyes.

The armored recovery vehicle, the hoverbus, and a badly damaged hovertank were before me.

My crew, my men, my faithful soldiers, stood staring at me.

"Mount the vehicles. I need a volunteer to drive the tank as I shall act as its gunner," I stated, trotting toward the tank.

The entire side was ripped open, exposing the crew cabin. I would not need to open the rear crew loading ramp.

"But, Most High, you will not be protected," Feelmeenta said, wringing her hands.

"It does not matter. This must be done, thus I shall be the one to do it," I told her.

"I will drive," a wounded Savashan told me. "I drove tanks from the motor pool to the maintenance bays as well as tested the drive trains after repair or refit."

"I will run your defensive systems," another told me, a Telkan with burn bandages down her side told me.

"Then we shall ride into defeat and glory together," I told them.

The inside of the tank stunk of burnt flesh as we climbed in. It started, the autoloader whined as it brought a plasma round from the munition storage into the chamber, the fans howled, and the entire thing vibrated.

It was wounded, mortally so, but could still fight.

My driver, Karelesh, rotated the tank and, at my direction, led our pathetic convoy out of the hastily assembled base and into the city.

"We should have reloaded the flares and chaff and smoke," the Telkan, Lu'ucilu'u, said softly as she activated the electronic counter-counter measures up and activated the wan and flickering battlescreens.

"Remember, if we encounter Precursor machines, we pull them away from the hoverbus," I ordered. "We may only be able to

buy them a few minutes, but those minutes may mean the differ-
ence between life and death for an entire busload of people."

"As you say, Most High," Lu'ucilu'u said.

I was chewing stimcud, my brain singing with that tight,
almost heard sound, that strange feeling that a wire inside your
mind has had too much tension put on it. I needed sleep, but there
was no time for it, too many depended on me.

We were on the third hab when high intensity lasers cracked
out, the high energy beams superheating the air that then collapsed back onto the near-vacuum with rippling snarling thunder.
The port side battlescreen flared, but held.

Karelesh spun the vehicle in place as I pushed my masked
face against the gunner's sight, lifting my hoof in readiness.

The machine was function over form, blocky and heavy, a
rotating barrel mining laser slicing at the tank with a continuous
beam of coherent light. It slid into my sight but the sight's elec-
tronics kept wavering and pixelating, telling me that there was no
target.

"SHOT OUT!" I snapped, training overriding my fear as my
mouth went dry and my tendrils curled protectively.

I stomped the firing lever.

The plasma round hit it dead center, washing it with protomatter fire.

The fire cleared and the mining machine still stood there.

Our weapons are almost useless! We are all doomed! the
words of the hysterical Most High floated up in my mind as I
clenched my jaws on my stimcud.

The targeting computer fought me as I tried to realign the
barrel and I reached out and slapped the override, sending the
VI back to it's storage and taking over the gun myself. I lowered
the barrel as Karelesh skidded the tank sideways, away from the
hoverbus, and the Precursor machine turned to follow us.

"SHOT OUT!" I yelled as I stomped the lever.

The plasma round hit just in front of the machine, the heavy
burst of matter-energy combination slamming into the ferrocrete
road in a bright flash at an angle.

The ferrocrete, liquified and then flash hardened by the heat of the plamsa round, crashed into the machine. Its battlescreens flared purple and collapsed.

"SHOT OUT!"

The third shot dug another chunk of the road out, the matter hitting the Precursor machine and caving in the large central structure.

It shot sparks and collapsed.

Even though the environmental hookups weren't engaged and I had been in my armor for nearly two days, I still had to urinate as we kept sliding to the side. I licked my lips and tendrils, my mouth dry, as our slide brought another Precursor machine into view.

I moved the barrel, still running it on manual, even as part of me paid attention to the way my lower right hand fired the coaxial gun mounted next to the main gun.

I stomped the bar twice in rapid succession.

The first shot hit the heavy groundcar, causing it to explode and lift up off the ground. My second shot hit the car again, slamming it into the Precursor machine.

I fired a third time into the twisted and burning wreckage.

Precursor battlesteel parts showered out of the twisted carnage.

"More Precursors! A lot more, Most High Ha'almo'or!" Lu'ucilu'u called out. "We're being locked up."

"Go through them!" I shouted, loading another round of high-energy plasma warshot into the tank. I changed channels.

"Mal-Kar, this is Ha'almo'or, do you read?" I asked.

"I hear you, Most High!" Mal-Kar shouted over the roar of the hoverbus's fans and the noise of the passengers.

"Get them to safety! We'll buy you the time!" I yelled. I changed channels. "Prepare to meet your ancestors," I told me faithful crew. "We do this because we must and there is no-one else."

No better beings existed than those two who rode with me, as no better beings existed than those that marched with you into your own personal hells.

The tank was moving at maximum speed when we slammed between two heavy cargo lifters, throwing them to the side. I managed to fire the main gun twice, the additional heavy plasma machineguns all on autonomous rapid-fire, the two heavy plasma rounds crashing into the ground to rake the Precursors we were suddenly mixed in with shattered pieces of ferrocrete.

Karelesh spun us in place, the skirt of a plenum chamber scraping the ground and throwing a fan of sparks behind us as I double-pumped the coolant into the chamber, forcing it to cycle on an empty chamber, and loaded a plasma round in half the time I should have, slapping the override for the gunnery system.

I was the gunner, not computers, not VI, **me**! I may have been only a Gunner Fifteenth Class, but by the Terran's Digital Omnimessiah and the Twelve Biological Apostles, it was **I** who would wield this mortally wounded beast's claws against the foe of all living things.

Alarms were wailing as I kept firing. Half of my shots hitting the ferrocrete street, slashing the mechs with shrapnel, some of them covering the mechs with burning plasma long enough for me to get another shot into them.

Lu'ucilu'u launched two EW drones in quick succession, one of them almost getting sucked into the tank's open crew space by a sudden backdraft, and sent them at the Precursors.

I reached out, slapped the override, and ramped their tiny microreactors into overload right as Lu'ucilu'u slammed her hand down on the self destruct button.

Both drones detonated, the microfusion detonation biting a huge chunk out of the Precursor ranks that Karelesh ground his teeth and drove us straight into.

My teeth were itching, my bones aching, my guts aching, as the tank's hoverfans roared and we moved straight into the burning smoke of the explosion.

Finally, a stomp on the loading lever brought nothing but a steady beeping.

We were out of ammo.

"Sound retreat," I ordered.

"Aye, Most High," Lu'ucilu'u said.

"As you command, Most High," Karelesh said, sounding exhausted.

The tank stunk of excrement, of burnt electro-propellant, of overheated molycircs, of urine, sweat, and fear. All three of us, our armor was pitted, cracked, and bubbled. I was blind on one side, either because my helmet had failed or my eyes were gone.

It didn't matter as we raced, billowing smoke, for the refugee point.

We had survived the night.

When the refugee point came into sight we heard it.

And the small part of me that was rejoicing at having survived shriveled and died.

HEAVY METAL INCOMING!

GO NOT SILENTLY

How to describe those three simple words? Do I tell you about how loud it was, roaring across every frequency, every audible sound range? Do I talk about how it roared from every speaker, every flat pane of macroplas and glasteel and armaglass as well as any flat surface thin enough to vibrate? Do I tell you how the three words were full of such malevolent fury that it made my Shavashan driver, Karelesh whimper in fear? Do I try to explain to you how it was, all at once, a threat, a promise, an offer of salvation and a warning of incoming devastation?

It was not, gentle reader, a simple empty statement put forth by emotionless computers. It was not empty of emotion and flat sounding. It roared and bellowed full of lemur rage, primate aggression, and purely Terran menace.

It told you: The Lemurs of Terra Are Coming and They Are Pissed.

Recordings, simulations, even high-fidelity recreations do not carry the sheer weight those three words carry when they are bellowed out to let a being know that the lemurs are coming with guns. There is something completely... human... about their three-word warning.

Human trading, diplomatic, and civilian vessels arrive quietly, with a sparkle of jumpspace energies.

The Terran War Machine arrives with a roar of hatred and an explosion.

Those three words had reduced more than one being into hanging their head, surrounded by their own waste, mumbling "the lemurs are coming" over and over to themselves as they shuddered with terror.

I had no time for such things.

Our tank was badly damaged, to put it mildly. Less than 32% of minimum recommended armor plating was left, half of the interior systems down, the crew spaces open to the outside in three places.

And completely out of ammunition.

The "refugee and rearming point" came into sight and I breathed a sigh of relief. I had been wracked by fears of the lemurs destroying the place with orbital strikes or even landing in order to tear apart the shelters and kill the refugees.

Instead, there were tanks being worked on, the robotic repair systems running on each of the ten repair bays, neo-sapients working at the jobs they had been trained on, ammunition being brought over from the safety pit I had ordered dug for the munitions I had taken from the lockers to be put into.

The tank slid to a stop, the skirts grinding on the asphalt. We had enough armor breaches that I could see around the tank quite easily. Which was a good thing, since the majority of the sensors were nothing but fused circuitry and melted alloys.

I was able to scramble out of the hole in the side that we had gone into battle with, somewhat ungainly, but I had left my dignity back with my modesty and my arrogance. I staggered and nearly fell when my hooves hit the ground and I realized that somehow I had lost not only one of my hoofshoes, but the hoof itself, landing on the soft flesh normally hidden and protected the hard material of my hoof.

When I limped over to the aid station I stopped and stared.

The neo-sapients that had started work there were still there, joined by even more. I saw two fillies working with them, one wearing the jewelry and clothing of a high ranking matron. The other was barely mature, her nervousness evident as she moved from patient to patient.

Around me were slings and cradles and beds and cots, all containing wounded people. A tanker who's eyes had been burned away along with the crests on the back of his head and neck. A Telkan missing an arm and burns across the same side of his muzzle and torso. A Savashan missing her tail and one leg.

And so many more.

I stood there, feeling a crushing feeling in my chest as I stared at all the wounded. The young filly made a low moan of pain before stepping away from a Tnvaru for a moment, then moving back to cover the Tnvaru's face with a cloth.

They had died. Despite all of my efforts.

The matron moved up to me, running the beam of the medical scanner over me.

"I can treat the minor burns and contusions and bruises if you take off your armor, but I should take care of your missing hoof first," she said.

"Just the foot, Matron," I said, limping to a sling.

I'd like to say I was stoic during the procedure, but I cried out in pain twice as she debrided the dead flesh, sprayed sealant on it, then wrapped it in a protective cast.

The painkillers were for those who were wounded worse than me.

And, of course, the dying.

While she was wrapping my foot Lu'ucilu'u came in, removing her helmet. Her fur looked slick, almost like plastic, and her whiskers just behind her little triangular nose were bent. She looked exhausted as she sat down next to me, out of the way of the matron working on my arm.

"Does it hurt, Most High Ha'almo'or?" she asked me.

"Very much," I admitted, wiping the tears from my face. "But it could be worse. We saw that it was worse for many."

She nodded slowly.

I looked at the Matron, shuddering with exhaustion. "I need something from you."

She raised one eyebrow.

"I need a shot of stimulant. I must return to my self-appointed task," I told her.

She frowned at me and I could see her looking at where the mechanics were using a winch to drag my much-abused tank to a repair cradle with her side eye. She lowered her head slightly and stared at me. "And how long have you been awake, 'Most High'?" she asked.

I knew right there that she knew I was no Most High and I sighed as I checked my datalink's chrono.

"Forty one point three two hours, Matron," I said softly.

She stared for a long moment. "You are the one who was protecting the bus that rescued my daughter and I, are you not?"

I nodded. "Yes, Matron," I said. She knew of my dishonor, knew that I was actually a prisoner that had just been deemed too minor and inconsequential to jail in the face of a Precursor assault.

She held up an injector, fiddling with it. "This injector contains powerful stimulants, Ha'almo'or," she said softly. "If I were to inject you, say, in your forward left flank, with this, you would feel your fatigue and hunger drop away for nearly twenty hours," she set it on the tray next to me. "I cannot in good conscious administer this injection, and I must warn you: you risk heart and brain damage should I inject you. It would put you in danger, you may very well suffer cardiac muscle damage, your lungs could fill with fluid, you could suffer blood clots in your brain," she turned away, closing her rear eyes. "Do not inject yourself, Ha'almo'or, and heed my warning and understand my reasons for not injecting you."

I nodded. "Of course, Matron, how foolish of me," I said softly.

Lu'ucilu'u's eyes burned like fire as I picked it up, stripped the safety cap off of it, and stared at it for a long moment.

I slammed the autoinjector into the thick muscle on my flank, ignoring the fact that it stung.

My heart started hammering and my chest filled with pain. I groaned and found that Lu'ucilu'u held my two left hands while Feelmeenta held my right hands. My breath came in painful gasps, feeling like glass was stabbing into me. My injured foot burned with pain, my eyes felt like they were going to explode in the sockets, and for a moment I thought I was going to die as the synthetic hormones coursed through my system.

Then it was past.

I closed my eyes and slowly opened them, the fatigue, the

numbness, the gnawing of hunger pains swept away.

Karelesh ducked into the tent, flinching slightly at the cries of pain and suffering, but moved over to me.

"We have another tank. The crew abandoned it and fled in a grav-lifter," he told me. "It is fully loaded with ammunition and the armor is unblemished."

I nodded, gently untangling the sling.

"We will go forth and save more people. How much more space do we have?" I picked up my helmet, the surface gray and pebbled from too many near hits.

"Enough room for nine thousand more. The technicians are working on the last two bunkers, if they finish while we rescue people, there will be enough room for fifteen thousand," he told me. He looked into the distance and I knew he was checking his datalink. "That's thirty trips with the bus."

"Any priority concentrations of civilians?" I asked, moving toward the tank that Feelmeenta was standing next to. She had painted "CIVILIAN PROTECTORATE SERVICES" on the side with an auto-painting drone.

"Two habs. Roughly three thousand living beings in the habs. A mix of species," Lu'ucilu'u said softly.

HEAVY METAL INCOMING! HOLD THE LINE, BROTHERS! roared out and many cried out in pain and fear as the sound echoed from hundreds of sources.

"We do not have long," I said. "Soon the Terran lemurs will be here," I pointed at the sky. "They will attack the Precursors and us. We must get the civilians to shelter."

"The Terrans have no reason to attack us," Julkrex, who had ridden with me and helped me run the guns that first terrible night, said softly. "They are here to kill the Precursors and only those who attack them."

"My people attacked theirs. They are at war with the Unified Species Council," I told him. I triggered the personnel ramp and watched it slowly unfold.

"Terrans are a strange people," Julkrex said. "If we do not attack them then perhaps they will not attack us."

"Pray to your benevolent digital deity," I told him, trotting up the crew ramp. "I will curse the names of the Forgotten Ones, the Gods that perhaps my people worshiped before we left them behind."

Julkrex joined us, getting into the secondary gunner position to take over on the secondary guns, including the mortars and missile launchers. Lu'ucilu'u got into the electronic warfare position, activating each system.

"At least this time we have chaff, flares, and drones," she said. "The mechanics are installing additional battlescreen projectors, the ones used for the heavy tanks."

"We will need them," I said. I loaded a round into the chamber on the plasma cannon, shuddering at the memory of how my first shot had been virtually ignored by the Precursor machine.

I had learned how to strike at them. Their battlescreen projectors were weak at the seams, the armor was vulnerable to kinetics and I could use the plasma cannon to strike at them with shrapnel.

The sun was rising as we entered the city, a red orb in the sky hidden by smoke and worse that filled the sky. It looked like a great bloody eye staring at us as we drove into the city. I was leading the massive hoverbus with my tank. Behind the bus was the wrecker and nearly a dozen cargo lifters driven by neo-sapients, some of them injured.

The immature filly was inside a cargo lifter marked with "EMERGENCY MEDICAL" in blue paint on the side, driven by a pair of Tnvaru, with four Telkan on the top of the box cargo area, all carrying plasma rifles dropped by fleeing infantry.

A Hamaroosa with a loud speaker called out to people we passed, urging them to follow the road to our refugee point, urging them to abandon the city as fast as possible. Many of them were weeping, staggering, many of them dressed in rags that had replaced their clothing.

One by one we began emptying houses, the habs, any building we could.

It was noon when I heard it over the communications bands.

The voice of A'armo'o, the Great Grand Most High.

"All commanders, perform a fighting withdraw toward the nearest populations centers. All infantry commanders who still command men, who are to be commended for their valiant actions and gallantry, are to sweep through the cities, creating fighting positions," the calm voice of the grand commander of armor stated. "All armored vehicles, move to the coordinates I have sent. We will create a fighting line around the population centers and seek to keep the Precursor machines away from the population as long as possible."

I breathed a sigh of relief as my tank hummed around me. We had grounded it, letting the guns cool, letting the slagged armor on the rear port flank cool, giving Lu'ucilu'u time to load in new algorithms for her EW systems.

My datalink clinked and pinged, a message coming in directly to me.

"Ha'almo'or, are you there?" the voice was A'armo'o, speaking directly to me again.

"Yes, Great Most High," I said, feeling awed. I rubbed my chest, working to banish the ache.

"I cannot spare you any forces for the task I have set you upon, this task you have shouldered yourself," A'armo'o stated. "How are your plans proceeding?"

"We have not rescued as many as I wish in the six hours since dawn," I told him truthfully. "Only six thousand living beings," I gave a slight shudder. "My medical center is overwhelmed, I have no doctors, only the medical kits from abandoned tanks and lifters, and I cannot save the badly injured. I am forcing them flank to flank, haunch to chest, into the shelters," I gave another shudder. "Most High, they all weep as I lock the door."

"You have rescued six thousand beings in six hours, Ha'almo'or?" he asked me.

"I have, Most High," I replied.

"You said it was not as many as you wish. How many did you wish to save?" He asked me.

"All of them," I admitted. "All of them, Most High. What use am I if I cannot save them?"

There was silence a moment.

HEAVY METAL INCOMING! MAKE WAY! roared out.

"Save the civilians, Ha'almo'or, as many as you can," Most High A'armo'o said softly. "Gunner Fifteenth Class Ha'almo'or, I am proud to call you, and those who labor with you, brother. A'armo'o out."

I sat for a moment, putting my face in my hands. I wanted to weep, my mind racing, my thoughts jumbled together, memories jangling in my brain.

The Terrans were coming.

HEAVY METAL IS HERE!

No. The Terrans were here.

"Soon, we will face the mad lemurs of Terra in addition to the Precursors," I said, reaching out and taking hold of the controls of my tank's massive main gun. "The vehicles are loaded, the hab has been emptied. We must return."

"We are nearly out of ammunition," Julkrex said.

"The battlescreen projectors are nearly burnt out, we have no spares to rotate in," Lu'ucilu'u stated.

"We will guard their rear," I stated.

HEAVY METAL IS HERE! roared out again.

I shuddered again, remembering that each roar was not a single ship, but rather an entire combat group of them. Dozens of them.

Armed to the teeth with weapons dangerous even to those who fired them and armored beyond reason to withstand even Precursors main battery fire.

It would have taken nearly an hour to reload the tank, the robotic systems working as fast as they could.

We simply moved to a new tank that Feelmeeta painted "EMERGENCY SERVICES" on the side again in blue paint.

The sun was high in the sky, but hidden, just a glimmering red circle in the sky that was hidden by smoke and ash, as we drove back into the city.

We did not listen to the channels, they were full of panic and dismay.

I was ashamed of my fellow soldiers as I saw them run by or drive by, their weapons and in some cases, even their armor, abandoned as they fled the battlefield.

"Where do they think there is to go?" Karelesh asked as he narrowly avoided hitting a fast infantry assault grav lifter full of panicked troops.

"Where there are no Precursor machines," Feelmeenta said quietly.

We were silent as we moved up to the last hab. We had two buses now, over a dozen heavy lifters, and nearly a score of infantry lifters, all of them containing armed neo-sapients.

Twice they had been forced to shoot panicked Lanaktallan troops who tried to take the lifter from them. Following my orders and shooting to kill, not wound, not maim, not frighten.

Shoot to kill was the phrase of the day.

We were heading back, following the wrecker, the lifters, when the starboard battlescreen gave a rippling snarl as the Precursor machines stormed out of a half-collapsed building.

I kept calling "SHOT OUT" reflexively as I stomped the firing bar as fast as I could convince the loader to slam ammunition into the chamber. Julkrex ran all three guns at once, his hands moving rapidly. Two hand operated and one slaved to his helmet visor. Karelesh kept us moving, dodging as many shots as possible, sliding us to the side.

He was pulling the Precursors to the side of the hover-bus's path, the path of the refugees.

The tank was taking hits, more and more. The forward battlescreen collapsed and Karelesh turned us around even as I spun the turret to keep the Precursors in sight.

"Battlescreen projector two reload jammed!" Lu'ucilu'u called out. "Trying to override!"

"SHOT OUT!" I answered, stomping the firing bar, converting an abandoned luxury limo into slashing shrapnel, the second shot pushing the shrapnel on a wave of superheated protomatter.

We took another hit, and another, and another. The gun was

beeping but I stomped the override and shut down the computer assist, running the gun by eye.

The front of a building crashed down as a Precursor machine ten times the size of my tank pushed through the bottom of the building.

I put a shot into its face, then a second.

Its return fire collapsed our battlescreen and ripped the armor off over the back deck. Particle beams vomited from a dozen cannons tore into us. Nacelle seven and eight's housing was vaporized and we scraped to stop. Another hit ripped enough armor off of the turret's starboard side that a hand's width gap appeared. Another hit and the tank spun as the massive energy transfer from the particle beam caused our armor to explode outward.

I stomped the bar and the computer refused to fire, the barrel snapped off only a meter from the armor of the turret.

I slapped the override and stomped again.

"SHOT OUT, DAMN YOU!" I bellowed.

"My friends, it has been a pleasure," Julkrex said, running the two remaining guns.

"I will see my family again soon," Lu'ucilu'u said.

"WE AREN'T DEAD YET!" I roared out. I reached up and tried to open the gunner's hatch. It was jammed and I slapped the emergency button. The hatch blew off on the explosive bolts and I stood up, poking my helmeted head out. I aimed by eyeball and fired again.

The plasma just washed over the massive machine.

It slowed and I could feel its cold malevolence.

It knew there was nothing we could do.

Another stomp and I heard the beeping telling me that the gun was empty.

There was no more ammo.

I reached down and grabbed my plasma rifle off the rack, lifting it up and aiming through the sight.

There was a roaring sound, a high pitched shrill whistling shriek with the roaring sound of thrusters right at the last second.

Explosions suddenly bracketed my tank as large objects

slammed into the ground. They were eight sided cylinders, a heavy retrothruster at the base surrounded by smaller guidance thrusters. They hit the ground, blowing tarmac and gravel into the air.

I kept firing at the Precursor machine, yelling at it.

No words, for I had none. Just maddened yelling and screaming that had no words, only sounds.

I would not go quietly into the darkness of death.

No.

Lanaktallan are silent when born. I had been quiet and silent all my life.

No more. Not now. Not in my last moments.

I would go out screaming like an insane lemur.

The sides of the objects dropped and out came nightmares.

The Mad Lemurs of Terra had arrived.

THE MAD LEMURS
OF TERRA

You may have seen Terran soldiers on documentaries or dramatizations. Fighting against the Unified Council, the Precursor Autonomous War Machines, the Atrekna, or even one another. In all of those, the Terrans talk. Terse orders from professional, dedicated, and experienced officers with clear cut mission goals, shouted commands from battle hardened non-commissioned officers to rally their men, order complex maneuvers, or direct the devastating firepower of the humans, or even the shouts, war cries, and enraged bellows of Terran soldiers caught up in combat.

It makes for fantastic imagery, but those words, those sounds, those commands, are all taken from records or written by a script writer and recorded. Their communications as well as what they say inside their armor is recorded and archived and used in dramatizations and documentaries.

On the battlefield, for the most part, the Terran Confederate Armed Forces fight in silence to those not connected to their Battlefield Tactical Network.

Which makes them all the more imposing.

Massive heavily armored beings, made huge in their power armor, almost a third against the height of a grown Lanaktallan stallion, twice as wide, their arms as thick as a Lanaktallan's upper leg, their legs massive foundations that root the galaxy's most fearsome intelligent tool using predator to the very ground they fight upon.

Their armor is all black, a light drinking matte black that somehow seems like it should be shiny. Bulky to the point they seem that they should be clumsy. Instead, they move fluidly, as if their power armor is merely another skin. Weapons are built into the armor, particle beam projectors, micro and mini-missiles, point defense systems, indirect fire weapons. They carry as much defenses as my tank: battle screen projectors, steri-field projectors, chaff, flares, micro-prism smoke, and more.

Their suits, contrary to dramatizations, are not blank. They have information for those who know where to look. Terran numbers on the shoulder, forehead, across their back, and on their chest, each set of numbers over a bar-code that allows their officers and NCO's to identify them almost instantly. On their right shoulder is the flash of a unit they have seen combat with. In the case of those who have seen combat with more than one unit, their favorite or the one with the most impressive lineage. On their left shoulder, the symbol of the Confederate Armed Forces underneath the flash of their current unit. Above the barcode and number on the helmet is their rank. Below their number on the left of their chest is their surname, their branch of service below that, and below that up to three specialized training. On the right is merely "TERRAN CONFED" for all to see.

The ones that landed had on their left shoulders what looked like a blue shield, with a Terran symbol for the number '8' in white and a yellow arrow piercing it from the bottom.

To a Lanaktallan, and many of the civilized, near-civilized, and neo-sapient species, it is a dizzying amount of information, but for a Terran it is all easily recognizable at a glance.

Think on that, gentle reader. In a split second a Terran has absorbed all the information given with a mere glance, even without accessing their datalink.

It took weeks for me to remember even where to look for the information I needed to know.

The sides of the orbital drop pods opened and terror walked out on two legs, their weapons readied, their targets locked in.

In complete silence a Terran from each pod directed fire from a harness mounted heavy gun into the front of the Precursors. Part of me expected the rounds to just bounce off or spark as they flattened.

The harsh blue-white actinic flare of antimatter roared to life as the shells tore apart the armored front of the Precursor vehicle. Two Terrans fired missiles before leveling fire from their weapons into the machines around the Precursor heavy vehicle. Their weapons smashed the Precursors into junk even as the antimatter tore at the mechanical entities that had slaughtered almost unopposed for three days.

The smoke, whitish blue, covered the area as one of them deployed masking munitions.

My tank shuddered as one jumped up next to me, bounding across nearly fifty paces in two short hops that left him crouched down next to me, one hand on the hull of my crippled tank, the other one holding out the compact weapon that was roaring as it fired heavy shells at the machines.

"Is your crew alive, Lanky?" his, if it was a he, asked in a heavily synthesized voice.

I made a motion of assent, my mouth suddenly too dry to talk. I managed to croak out a 'yes' and the helmet nodded.

"Good. The Miss Daisy's intel section spotted you from orbit about to lock horns with that thing. Sorry it was at the last second but it took a few minutes to get here," they told me.

"You are not here to destroy me?" I asked. My body was shaking, the adrenaline and the stimulant shot almost too much for me. The Precursor machine gave an almost biological scream as the superstructure collapsed in on itself.

A Terran fired a rocket into the burning wreckage.

The helmet moved side to side. "No. Not unless you shoot at us on purpose," they told me. "How badly are your men wounded?"

"We're... we're all right for now," I told him. I felt a sudden rush of shame when I realized the Terrans had destroyed, with apparent ease, a Precursor machine that my tank had been ineffective against.

"There's what looks like a forward operations base behind you, about four miles. Can you make it or is your tank inop?" the Terran asked.

I looked at my tank and shook my head. "My tank is destroyed."

"There's a recovery vehicle nearby. Are you in contact with it?" the Terran asked.

I nodded again.

"You'll be all right here. I'm going to leave a three man fireteam. There's a refugee convoy leaving the city and I have orders to protect it," the Terran said. They stood up and looked down at me. "Sorry about your tank, you poor brave bastard."

With that they leaped away, landing easily next to where the rest of the Terrans had gathered up.

I put my hand to my helmet and activated my comlink.

"Mal-Kar, do you read?" I said. My datalink communications were full of pops, clicks, and bursts of static.

"I read you, Most High," Mal-Kar said. I could tell by the relative quiet that he was had taken over driving the armored recovery vehicle, passing the bus to another.

"My tank is disabled. I need recovery," I told him.

"I have your beacon. Ten minutes," he said. He paused for a moment. "There are Terrans in power armor here, on our flanks. They are not attacking us, only the Precursor machines. Other than that, they do nothing but march."

"Ignore them unless they give you a command for your own safety and the safety of our charges," I ordered. "Ha'almo'or, out."

"Mal-Kar, out," he said.

I looked over at the three Terrans that had been left behind. One had a heavy gun in some kind of harness, the linked belt of ammunition connecting the gun to a pack on the back of the power armor. As I watched three of five fins withdrew into the armor. The other two had heavy rifles as well as the compact fully automatic weapons on one hip with a large cutting bar on the other.

The infamous Terran chainsword AKA Cutting Bar Mark Two.

I watched as one of them deployed two drones, small things with mylar wings. They chuffed out, shooting into the air, and unrolled, becoming nearly invisible as they began to glide around us.

I had never seen a Terran before. I knew I still was not, I was only seeing their armor, but I couldn't help but stare.

They looked like the universe's malevolence made manifest.

Finally Mal-Kar arrived and I got out of the tank, shaking with near exhaustion, and helped attach the hooks on the ends of the cables to the lift points on my crippled tank. It took nearly two minutes to winch the tank into place, attach the graviton lifters, and for my crew to get into the recovery vehicle.

I sat on the damaged and destroyed back deck, my plasma rifle in my hands, watching as we left the city.

"Gunner Ha'almo'or, this is Most High A'armo'o, do you read me?" came over my comlink.

"Affirmative, Most High," I said.

"The Terrans are landing in your position. I have spoken to one of their leaders and they will be reinforcing your refugee point. The Terrans are, for right now, on our side," A'armo'o said. His voice was deep and calming. "I have agreed to meet the Terran tank commander face to face soon, and have spoken to his commander, a General No'Drak. The Terrans have agreed to work with you."

"Yes, Most High," I said.

"Do what you must do to save the civilians, Ha'almo'or," his voice was solemn.

"I will, Most High, I promise," I answered.

"I know you will," his voice had an odd note to it. "A'armo'o, out."

"Ha'almo'or, out," I answered.

I sat on the back deck, staring at the city around me. It was badly damaged, smoke rising from a hundred points, houses and office buildings and even factories burning. From the direction of the starport black smoke rose in a massive cloud that reached to the skies before flattening out.

We passed corpses. Most of them were my fellow Lanaktallan soldiers, killed while trying to flee.

But there were civilian bodies.

Too many. Much too many.

Four times I ordered Mal-Kar to stop, climbing down, my cast thumping on the plascrete, to check to see if they were dead.

Under a dead Telkan broodcarrier four pair of eyes stared at me, blinking, holding tight to the blood crusted fur of their mother.

I gathered them carefully, putting them in an empty box that had held rations forever ago. They were quiet, just staring with wide eyes.

I hoped that at least one of their other two parents had survived, but the carnage where a handful of Precursor machines had found fleeing civilians gave me little hope.

Less than a half mile one of the three Terrans made a hand-signal at me. I ordered Mal-Kar to stop the vehicle and climbed down.

"Yes?" I asked, nervous. We were exposed, the buildings around us burnt out husks.

"There are six Akltak life-signs under that destroyed hovertruck. They appear to be immature chicks," the Terran said. I noted that the synthesized voice was the same as the other one that had spoke to me.

It gave me the chills.

The Terrans were faceless, identical in voice and features. Kill one, another identical one took its place. The message was simple: "We are unyielding."

Still, I pushed away my fears, moving over and kneeling down, lowering my torso to look under the hovertruck.

Little eyes looked back.

It took me several minutes to lure them out, the Terrans staying back. One brought a box nearby and set it down, backing up.

They all looked like three black statues.

The little moltlings huddled in the box, not even peeping, and I covered them with some camouflage netting before passing them to one of the civilians inside the recovery vehicle.

At one point a handful of Precursor machines roared by overhead. For the last two days they had owned the skies, hunting and killing at will, with nobody to stop them.

This time they were heavily pursued by three blocky and unfinished looking grav-strikers flanked by a dozen flying power armors on each side.

They had stopped firing as they came close, but resumed as they passed over us. Heavy shell casings fell from the sky, a waste of bronze as the shells rained from the sky to dance and chime on the pavement.

The Precursors ruled the skies no more.

The lemurs had arrived, with fire and thunder and steel.

Two blocks later we saw a strange sight. Two immature Tukna'rn, still large and muscular, were pushing a ground car limousine being steered by a Plekit who was sitting on a plas crate, with a Cemtrary sitting on the front seat, where the door had been ripped away, holding a stun-stick normally carried by Law-Sec.

One of the Terrans broke into a jog, catching up. The two Tukna'rn nodded, their faces covered with sweat, and climbed onto the trunk.

The Terran started pushing the vehicle effortlessly, easily keeping up with the recovery vehicle.

I saw over a dozen heads poke up from one of the back seats before a Ikeeki hand pushed them back down.

All children.

We made another three stops before reaching the refugee point. Each time they joined us. Once a ground car was being pulled by a dozen Telkan that had attached chains to the front end and were pulling the chains, dragging the car behind them while a Plekit drove.

They had all heard that safety was just a little ways further down the road.

I prayed that it still was.

My chest ached, a dull burning pain in my upper torso, but I ignored it as the recovery vehicle dragged my poor dead tank into the lot and toward the repair bay.

I climbed down, standing and watching as the two vehicles,

both them knocked out by an EMP days ago, were pushed by Terrans into the lot.

Part of me shriveled inside of me at the memory of how many dead I had seen.

"Get me another tank," I told Karelesh, staring at the city we had just left. "There are those who still need us."

"As you command, Most High," he said, turning and moving away toward the line of tanks that sat neat and orderly, having been abandoned by those fleeing the battle.

"Pardon me, are you the officer in charge?" A Terran asked, moving up to me. This one was in hard plate armor, the faceplate of the visor was clear and I could see their face. I did not know if they were male or female, but their close set eyes burned with a predator's stare.

"There are no officers, only me," I stated. "The others were killed," I paused for a moment. "Or ran."

The Terran nodded. "Then you're it until I find someone higher ranking, someone better, or you get killed," they said. They held out a hand. "I'm Lieutenant Colonel Jessica Martin Laverty, One-one-nine Combat Sustainment Battalion. We're here to assist you, General No'Drak's compliments."

I thought for a moment. "What does a Combat Sustainment Battalion do?"

The Terran explained quickly. They kept combat units in the fight, rapidly repairing or rearming entire brigades, providing medical care for the wounded, and keeping supplies flowing. An entire company of medical, another company of mechanics, a company of ordnance, supply, fuel, heavy vehicle operation, weapon maintenance, communications, a platoon of electronic warfare specialists, and a company of light powered infantry.

When they said light powered infantry, they waved at the two heavy power armor soldiers standing near me.

Only Terrans would consider a half ton suit of power armor to be 'light powered infantry.'

"Our Ordnance tech, Sergeant First Class Grist, says that you've got a nice dug in spot to start fabbing up munitions for your tanks," the Terran said. They waved toward the pit I'd ordered dug to store the plasma rounds. "She's setting up a nanoforge right now. She copped the specs for your ammo by scanning a few of your rounds and a few of your tank main guns."

The Terran stared at me for a long moment.

"Your current ammo is next to useless. You can't fight them with it," they said.

I nodded. "I have adapted a strategy that works against many."

The Terran gave a slow nod. "Be that as it may, if you give my men twenty minutes, we can fix that. I've got some of the best Ordnance techs in Eighth Infantry Division right here."

"I will take any help you can give," I said. "My priority is to get the civilians to safety."

"Eight-Two-One Combat Engineers are working with your people right now. They're digging shelters and assembling them as fast as possible. They'll survive an orbital strike," the Terran paused. "Whoever turned those ammo lockers into shelters was smart. They're designed to handle atomic or orbital strikes. They won't be comfortable, but they'll do the job."

"I thank you," I told her. "I did not know what else to do."

The Terran stared at me for a long moment. "Do you mind if I ask your military occupation?"

"I am a Gunnery Specialist Fifteenth Class, specializing in tank main gun weaponry," I said. I waved my hand at my surroundings. "All of this, I just guessed."

The Terran nodded again. "You did well."

I held up my cast, which was dark with blood. "I must see a medical personnel about my foot. I have bled through the cast."

The Terran stared at me. "You aren't like other Lankys, are you?"

I made a non-committal motion. "I am simply one of the Great Herd."

The conversation seemed over so I limped to the medical tent. When I pushed my way in I stopped and stared.

Before it had been chaos. Medical supplies had been non-existent, only slings and what medical kits we could scavenge out of vehicles.

Now Terrans in their uniforms moved through the patients. The Matron now wore a type of uniform that made her look official, and she was leaning down to watch a Terran work quickly with a device that stripped away burnt flesh and fur and left behind gleaming pink tissue. The younger filly was being talked to by two Terrans in silverish-gray power armor that had a red crescent on one side of the chest and a red cross on the other. They were showing her tools and giving some kind of instruction before putting them in the satchel the filly carried.

The Matron saw me as I removed my helmet. She made an excuse to the Terran and moved over, looking down.

"You have bled through your cast, Most High," she said. She touched my neck, her fingers finding the artery there. "Your heart is racing, you are sweating, and your pupils are constricted."

"We were nearly killed," I admitted. "Luckily, the Terrans arrived in time to provide assistance."

She nodded, looking solemn and regal, despite the fact she no longer wore the sash, vest, flank covering, and jewelry of a noblewoman.

"I will have the doctor examine your foot, Most High," she said. She put one hand on my armored chest. "What you do here, it may not be remembered by history, but there are many who will remember your actions."

"And many who will not," I said softly. "Too many."

"You cannot save them all, Most High Ha'almo'or," she said gently. "You can only save those you can, and you have saved many who were abandoned."

I nodded, feeling emotions I did not understand well up inside of me.

Thankfully, the Terran medical specialist came over at that time.

"I am Specialist Grade-Six Eleonore Michael Chidi, a Field Medical Specialist," they said. Again, I did not know if it was a male or female. "Where are you wounded?"

"My foot has bled through my cast," I stated, pointing down.

The Terran looked down at my foot. "Scan him, we'll treat that foot first unless his armor is hiding anything life threatening."

It was not, although the Terran insisted I remove my armor. When I broke the environmental seal the stench of scorch and burnt hair and hide assaulted my nostrils. My left flank was covered in small pinprick scabs from when the interior of the tank had exploded into us and pieces of battlesteel had penetrated my armor.

The Matron and the Medical Specialist Grade Six smeared glittering clear gel on my flanks, then went to work on my hoof. Pain I was only vaguely aware of receded as whatever the gel was did its work. The Terran gave me an injection in my foot that relieved the pain but did not deaden my foot.

They were almost done when a Terran came in, carrying new armor.

"Compliments of Lieutenant Colonel Laverty and the Battalion Armorer," the Terran said. "It's virtually identical, just better laminate armor and kinetic shock packs."

"Thank you, Terran," I said.

I meant it.

Despite the Matron's objections, I put on the new armor and limped out into the wan sunlight of the dying day.

Grav-strikers roared by overhead, flanked by air-mobile power armor.

The Terrans were all moving quickly, purposefully, in some cases running from place to place. Construction machines roared, the tanks were being worked on by Terrans as well as the robotic systems, and I could see a conveyor line moving new tank rounds to the tanks being fixed.

The Terran commander walked up, their movements assured and brisk.

Part of me wished I could move with such assurance and authority.

"There's a tank loaded and refit for you, Most High," the Terran said. I looked at her, wondering if they was joking. I had told them my rank, but instead, they spoke to me as if I was a peer. They saw my look and shrugged. "This is your base, your people call you Most High, out of respect I will use the rank they feel comfortable with."

They gave me a long, serious look. "I would prefer if you stayed here, to remain in command of this forward operations base," They turned and looked at the city, which burned and filled the sky with smoke then turned and they watched a podling being carried by an Ikeeki who's feathers were scorched. The podling's eyes were wide, the fur of their face damp with tears as they clutched tightly to the avain. "However, I understand what you are feeling."

Their eyes grew far away, shadowed with a pain I did not understand.

Or rather, I had come to understand all too well.

"This isn't the first city I've seen burn. When I was a little girl, the Mar-gite attacked my world. I saw the city of my birth burning as I was evac'd out. As an adult, I've seen cities burn, but I remember none of them as clearly as I remember shining Vulmera burning with white fire," their voice was full of something that I suddenly understood.

Regret and loss.

"Carry on with your mission, Most High Ha'almo'or," they said. They paused for a long moment. "The Terran Confederacy will support your mission to the best of our ability."

The podling's eyes followed me as I limped toward another tank.

JUST ONE MORE

We drove back into the city, myself and my companions in a tank loaded with new Terran munitions, my faithful crew in the recovery vehicle, others who had chosen, for some maddened reason, to follow me into the city driving two of the mass transit vehicles and a score of grav-lifters. The grav-lifters were sporting new weapons, the pintle mounted plasma machineguns previously arming those craft having been dumped into "grinders" and replaced with Terran kinetic weaponry. The grav-lifters sparkled with battlescreens, powered by a reactor sitting in the back, just as my tank wavered behind Terran light tank battlescreens.

The wailing of the damned could be heard even through the hull as we drove into the smokey ruins of the city. The entire planet was burning, the Precursor machines having forced the Great Herd back until their backs were pressed against the ferrocrete walls of the buildings. The communications net was full of Most Highs panicking as Terrans made landfall, sometimes into Great Herd fire, their soldiers and combat machines attacking the Precursors without mercy or hesitation.

A platoon of light powered infantry was with me to protect those I rescued.

To my surprise there were several flight capable power armors, all in flat gray, with a red crescent on one side of their chest and a red cross on the other, moving with the makeshift ambulance that now glimmered with battlescreens and sterifields. To either side of us bounded huge cybernetic creations. Goodboi's and Simbas, they were called. Canine and feline brains, respectively, in heavy combat chassis capable of fighting the Precursors as well as sniffing out survivors buried under rubble.

And there was so much rubble.

The recovery vehicle used its equipment to pull aside rubble and chunks of buildings. I saw Terrans in armor wade into the rubble, using the strength provided by their power armor to throw aside the rubble. I saw Goodbois stand on top of rubble and bark, calling out that they had found survivors.

Each Simba and each Goodboi carried packs of Purrbois, another cyborg, these polymorphic alloy chassis wrapped around a feline brain. The purrbois descended into the rubble, oozing through the slightest cracks. They provided medical care when necessary and alerted us to the living and dying.

Several times I got out of my tank to help pull people from wreckage, helping move rubble, helping hold back debris. I watched the Terrans wiggle into holes barely large enough to fit them in order to talk to the person we were rescuing. Purrbois were curled up on the chests of those trapped when we managed to reveal them, subsonic rumbling calming them and their injuries treated as best the tiny cyborg could manage.

Late in the afternoon, as the sun was lowering, I stumbled climbing down from the rubble. My cast caught wrong and I almost tumbled, caught and steadied by one of the power armor clad Terrans. I managed to limp back to my tank, my leg aching. I broke into the medical kit and got out a painkiller, dry swallowing them, and looked over my scanners.

THERE IS ONLY ENOUGH FOR ONE! echoed out.

The Terrans raised their voices in defiance: **THEN DIE ALONE!**

But still we worked.

There were still more emergency calls, emergency signals, all over the city. I could hear their wailing, crying out for help, even through the tank's armor.

The Terran concept of "Hell on Earth" had come to us.

I was sweating, the hatch open and half out of it, as we moved deeper into the city. Flames whipped up around us as we passed streets that had been torn open. A skyraker gave a loud groan, like a dying animal, and collapsed to the street.

The life signs calling for aid there suddenly winked out and I wanted to weep.

Still, we headed into the destroyed streets, my tank pushing rubble out of the way, the tracked recovery vehicle and I forging a path for the rest to follow.

The smoke was so thick that it was like night, thick enough to make the battlescreens snarl. Even with the filters in my suit my mouth and nostrils felt thick and greasy, I could taste the tang of burning metal and scorched meat.

We pushed on regardless, the Terrans assisting in finding just one more group of survivors.

Just one more.

That's all I wanted, just one more, as we drove through the streets of a murdered city.

Just before the dim red orb of the sun slipped below the sky-line of the city I was helping carry surviving children, hidden in shipping containers by a Lanaktallan warehouse manager, to the flitters, when the snarl and crack of Precursor lasers sounded out.

I took a hit on the flank, stumbling, as the armor shed the sudden energy transfer with a flare of light. A kinetic round hit the side of my helmet and I almost went down, hugging the box of Hashenesh squirmlings tight to my armored chest. The light and sound made them start slapping their tails against the bottom of the box and make little barking squeaks even as they huddled together.

I was staring at their wide eyes as I stumbled down the wreckage, heading for my tank, my head swimming, my thoughts incoherent and disconnected.

A Terran in a suit of light powered armor interposed his body between the three Precursor machines targeting me and the squirmlings in my arms.

I felt a weird sensation, like tape being pulled from my skin, around my ankle, where the cast was, but kept moving. I stumbled to the flitter and held up the box. The Kivyan inside was trilling in fear, her feathers ruffled, even as she took the box from me.

Two kinetic rounds hit my back, bouncing off my armor.

When I turned and looked, I could see the Precursor machines were approaching us from under a bridge overpass, advancing on us rapidly. The Terrans were putting up a fierce defense, but they were out of position, all to many of them holding children and infants.

I galloped for my tank, scrambling inside.

"FIRE IN THE HOLE!" I yelled out over the tank's loudspeakers even as I turned the turret, trying to get into position even as I scrambled over the gunner's couch.

The shot lined up.

"SHOT OUT!" I warned.

And stomped the fire bar.

The shot hit the bottom of the bridge/overpass and it collapsed with a roar, thousands of tons of ferrocrete thundering down on the Precursors.

I knew it wouldn't kill them, but it would delay them, give the Terrans time to regroup, time to get the survivors into the flitters and the buses.

"SHOT OUT!" I fired again, just for good measure.

There was silence, just the background wailing, the cracking of burning synthetics, and the groaning of stressed ferrocrete and alloy structural beams.

I rested against my sight, closed my eyes, and sighed.

There were so many left.

I wanted to go back out, help more, but when I stood up pain washed up my leg. I looked down and saw that my cast was missing, pulled free from my ankle and leg. My soft inner foot was resting against the armored floor of the tank, a pool of blood slowly seeping out.

I felt ashamed that I was unable to stand up, the pain too much for me.

As night fell we had emptied the last of the large buildings that were still intact, taking the survivors back to the refugee point. Repeatedly, off in the distance, there was the flash of atomic weaponry as the military clashed with the Precursors. Craft roared overhead, sometimes Precursors pursued by Terran craft, other times low flying Terran craft, sometimes Terran air mobile power armor.

When I parked, I managed to stumble out, limping, and help guide the refugees to the medical station or the bunkers.

People were afraid. Afraid of me, afraid of my people, afraid of the tank, afraid of the Terrans. Afraid of the lights and sounds of distant combat. Afraid for themselves, for their families, for their neighbors.

I pushed it away. I hardened myself against their pleas to not march them into the lifters and buses. I shut each door personally, staring at them as the heavy blast door closed in their faces.

I heard their pleas, their sobbing protests, and their weeping cries to not lock them in.

I had to.

THERE IS ONLY ENOUGH FOR ONE! roared out as I closed the doors.

THEN DIE ALONE! came the enraged roar back.

It was after dark and I was beginning to feel tired. My bones hurt, my head hurt, my muscles ached, and my chest had a dull burning ache through it. I couldn't seem to get enough air into my lower lungs no matter how deep I gasped and my all four of my hands shook as I gripped the controls of my gun, my eyes blurred as I watched through the scope. I was out of stimcud, the shot was wearing off, and my fatigue was catching up with me.

The Matron refused to give me a stim-shot. She wrapped my foot, my leg, chiding me. She attempted to convince me to stay, to be one of the wounded, but I refused.

My cast thumped as I walked out, ignoring her demands that I return.

I couldn't stay in the medical tent. The cries of the wounded, the moans of the dying.

The silence of the dead.

I staggered out and leaned against the tank, crying tears of frustration, banging my helmet against the tank's thick armor to banish the wailing from the city that was still audible.

THERE IS ONLY ENOUGH FOR ONE! screamed out, echoed

across the sky, making the psychic filters in my helmet clamp down hard enough my sensitive ears hurt as they were pressed against my skull.

THEN DIE ALONE! was roared back.

I thumped my head against the armor, trying to drive the thoughts out.

"You OK, Lanky?" a human stopped and put their hand upon my lower spine. "You've got an impact streak on your helmet."

"They need me, Terran," I said. I pointed at the city, which was still burning, lighting up the sky, adding its own light to the burning clouds above us, adding to the ash that drifted down around us.

The Terran nodded. "Get in. I'll get the platoon, we'll make another run," they said. The voice was too synthesized for me to tell if they were male or female.

"I cannot," I admitted. I thumped my helmet against the tank.

"517, check his helmet," the Terran said. they patted my back. "It's all right. I'm here with you. You can ride in the flitter if you can't ride in your tank."

I was dimly aware of something climbing up my back.

--damaged will fix-- appeared on my visor.

THERE IS ON... started.

It suddenly cut off.

--fixed-- the words appeared. I looked over in time to see an armored little foot tall mantid jump from my head to the Terran's shoulder.

"Better?" the Terran asked me.

I nodded, still feeling exhausted.

The Terran looked around, giving the feeling of slyness despite the fact that I couldn't see their face. "Look, man, I shouldn't do this, but get your crew, get in the tank, I'll get you a stim."

"What? How?" I asked them.

"Through the power of requisitioning equipment and supplies without proper paperwork and authorization due to emerging field expedient needs regarding the current theater and active operational tempo and operation operations," the Terran said as they headed toward the medical center.

I put the confusing words out of my mind as I slapped the panel and the back deck lowered so I could climb into the tank. My legs trembled as I lowered myself onto the gunner's couch before the seat back swung into place and I could buckle myself in.

I envied, for a moment, the Terran tankers. Being bipedal they did not require extensive seating, took up half the space, and could make do with much less space much easier with much more support and protection that I had.

But, to be honest, it didn't matter. I had something I had to do and I wasn't going to let something like discomfort stop me.

Using my helmet's radio I contacted my loyal crew and ordered them back into the vehicles.

Before anyone else arrived the Terran ducked into my tank, moving forward in an awkward way, shuffling up next to me.

"Don't ask," was all they said, taking my wrist and pulling my arm toward them. When my hand got close I opened it.

The Terran dropped three stim-sticks into my hand.

"Don't die. I'd give you a piece of stimgum but it would probably kill you," the Terran said. They shuffled in a half circle and waddled out of the tank. The little mantid waved from his back.

My fingers shook as I stripped the safety plug from the injector. It took me two tries to get the injection port open on my armor, but I managed. The injection felt like cold lava coursing through my veins. I could hear a high pitched ringing noise, feel my limbs shake, and a great pain and pressure descended upon my upper chest. I moaned, hanging loose in the restraining straps, shuddering and shaking as the stimulant coursed through my veins.

Mal-Kar got in just as the pain eased up and I sat up.

"Are we going back in?" he asked me.

I nodded. "We must. There are still more trapped who need us," I told him.

He just nodded.

My tank led the way as we moved back into the burning

city, the darkness of the night replaced by the hellish glow of the flames.

WHAT DO LIMITS MATTER?

My vision was blurred, my hands shaking, a ringing in my ears, and it was hard to breathe when we pulled into the refugee point just as dawn was breaking. In the distance the sky glowed with the violence of combat, flashes of atomic weaponry lighting up the dawn, outshining the sun, every few minutes. The ash was thick raining down from the sky, full of heavy metals and worse, my tank's scanners full of fuzz and distortion.

Mal-Kar brought the tank in and lowered it to the ground before turning off the hover fans.

The forward starboard fan made a clanging noise as it slowly wound down.

All three of my faithful crew were staggering as we climbed out of the tank. My vision kept going grey, shot with static, and at first I thought it was my helmet, that perhaps the Terran molycircs had failed.

No.

It was my eyes, my brain.

I stumbled twice before I found myself supported between two Terrans in body armor.

"Easy now, Most High, we've got you," the one on the right said. The first un-synthesized voice I had heard from a Terran. It was soft, gentle, but I still didn't know if it was male or female.

"Need to reload the tank. Go back out," I mumbled. My cast thumped against the tarmac.

"Let's get him to medical. Can you understand what he's saying?" the other one asked.

"He's asking about his tank, I think," the first one answered.

"You're tank's good. The mechanics will have it fixed right up by the time you get done with medical," one promised.

"There's more civilians. They need rescued," I mumbled.

We pushed into the medical tent. I shuddered at the contents. Injured people, some missing limbs, sobbing in pain as Terran doctors, the young filly, and the Matron moved through them, giving medical care where they could.

"Put him in sling seven," one of the Terrans said, pointing.

"There's still more out there. Just give me a stim," I said softly as the Terrans put me in the sling.

The Matron moved up, clicking her tongue in disapproval. She ran the scanner over me and her tendrils curled.

I struggled feebly against the sling, then went limp, exhausted. The front of my lower abdomen burned and ached, I couldn't catch my breath. She attached an IV line to my foreleg and another to my arm, shaking her head the entire time.

A Terran moved up in body armor, stopping next to the Matron. "Diagnosis?"

I expected the Matron to speak out loud, instead she just showed the dataslate to the doctor.

"Just patch me up, I need to get out there," I mumbled, looking up for a moment before looking back down, exhausted.

"You let us worry about that," the doctor said. He reached out and touched the complex device under the bag of simple saline water. It beeped and flashed a few lights. He turned to the Matron. "Tell his men it's just treatment for exhaustion and stimulant overdose."

The Matron nodded and trotted away. The doctor looked at me.

"Your mid-body heart is failing. Another hour and you would have started dying," he said. He put his hand on my armored forehead. "We're going to get you out of that armor, then I'm going to start working."

"There are others more wounded than me," I said, looking over at a HiKruth juvenile missing the legs on his right side. "What about him?"

"He's fine. He needs some regen time or a cloned tissue replacement," the doctor said. "You worry about you, Most High."

I tried to object, but the dark pulled me down.

I had expected to be unconscious for days, perhaps weeks, receiving treatment, but I woke up after less than fourteen hours, pulled to wakefulness by the dull roar and echoing rumble of an atomic detonation nearby.

Feelmeenta sat next to my bed, her arm in a sling, a patch covering her eye with black durachrome around the patch. When I raised my head she looked up at me, giving me a pleased expression.

"Welcome back, Most High," she smiled.

My head hurt and my chest felt weird, like it was packed with cotton.

"Get me out of this sling," I said, reaching for the buckles but finding my hands too clumsy and numb to do much more than fumble at the latches.

Feelmeenta shook her head. "No can do. The Terrans were very specific that you spend another six hours in that sling while the quikheal takes hold."

"But the civilians," I started to say.

"Where you led, others have followed," she told me. She put one hand on my paper gown covered flank. "The Terrans are helping with the effort."

The led to me sagging in the sling and beginning to weep.

My failure was complete.

Feelmeenta put her hand on my flank again. "It's OK, Most High. It's OK."

I went to sleep again, the drugs pulling me back under and back to sleep.

I woke up again, feeling the fuzziness of the anesthetic retreat slightly. My muscles felt better, no longer aching. My joints no longer felt like they were filled with a dull burning fire. My chest and lower abdomen no longer ached and my breathing came easy.

"How are you feeling?" Mal-Kar asked me from where he was sitting on an ammo can next to my sling.

"Better," I said. I swallowed thickly. "Water?"

Mal-Kar nodded, holding up a brown pitcher with a straw in it. "It's citrus flavored. Go slow."

I wanted to gulp it all down. It tasted amazing, better than anything I had ever tasted. The bite of the citrus seemed to clear the thick gummy taste from my mouth, wash away the strange taste of some kind of berry or fruit that I'd never tasted before.

I was only allowed three swallows before Mal-Kar pulled it back.

"How... how long?" I asked.

"Twenty hours," he told me. "The humans, the Terrans, have landed in force. They're driving the Precursors back across all fronts. Most High A'armo'o has ordered the Great Herd to interlock with the Terrans until further notice," he wiped his hands on the paper jumpsuit he wore over his mechanic's coveralls. "We're seeing less deserters."

"That's good," I said. I blinked, aware that only four of my eyes seemed to work.

Mal-Kar shrugged. "Means anyone not willing to fight is dead, ran away, or the officers got neural prods."

The doctor pushed in, the Matron looking around him. Again, I was struck how a Terran could be taller than me yet give the impression of being short and squat, despite the fact that he was lean enough to remind me of the knives carried by the bangers in the hab I'd grown up in.

"Good, you're awake. Your neural scans look good, but lets check for memory loss or any other neural defects," the doctor said.

The testing took only a few minutes. A few passes with a scanner, a few questions, looking into all four of my working eyes and my ears and up my nose. He tested my feeding tendril response, nodding slowly.

"All right, I'm going to turn on your two new eyes. They're Terran cybernetics, but they've been proven to work just fine for your people," he said. "They'll feel weird."

"Do we have time for me to be able to use the eyes?" I asked.

"Shouldn't take more than an hour or so for them to fully synch up. Most of the work was done while you were asleep," he said.

"Doctor..." the Matron said.

"I know. Just a few more minutes, I'd like to have his implants working," the doctor said.

My vision suddenly came back on my left rear arc. The logo "SYNTEK CYBERNETIC DIVISION" popped up then faded.

"Blink for me," he said. I did so and he nodded. "Focus on Nurse Cha'apehl," he said, pointing at the Matron. I did so. "OK, follow the light," he moved a light around. "All right. It's a non-cosmetic version. You can get it replaced by a cosmetic version or bioware implant later," he straightened up. "He can be released afterwards," he told the Matron. "Send him in."

The Matron nodded and Mal-Kar stood up.

"I should go," my faithful crewman said.

"Please, stay," I said, reaching out and grabbing his hand. I could see the shiny skin around my arm, where fur had not grown back, had replaced the surface burns on my arm.

Mal-Kar sat down.

The curtain parted and Great Grand Most High A'armo'o entered the tent. He was wearing his jeweled and ornate sash and flank covering, both festooned with awards, ribbons, recognition. His pistol on his belt was inlaid with precious metals and gems. His jewelry was shined and polished.

I felt my lip curl in disgust at the obvious finery he was prancing about in.

"You have seen the dark side, Gunner Ha'almo'or," he said. He tapped his chest. "They disgust you now, do they not?"

"They do," I admitted, and hung my head, embarrassed that I'd felt such a thing, dared to judge someone so very much my superior.

Most High A'armo'o leaned forward and whispered to me conspiratorially. "They disgust me too."

I felt my tendrils curl in embarrassment.

"Do you know why I am here?" he asked me.

Mal-Kar rubbed my newly healed forearm with his hand.

"No, Great Grand Most High," I answered, staring at the floor. "To place me back under arrest and remand me to LawSec?"

There was silence for a long moment.

"I have fought across the continent for three days, Ha'almo'or," he said solemnly. "Do you know how many civilians I directly saved in those three days?"

I shook my head. "No."

"None."

I looked up and Most High A'armo'o put his hand on my paper gown covered chest, holding my gaze with his own.

"I, and my men, fought as hard as we could," he said. "Would you like to hear what I told my men, all of the tankers of the Great Herd still surviving, upon the second day?"

I nodded, my mouth dry. I swallowed thickly and Mal-Kar held up the pitcher. I gratefully drank as Most High A'armo'o placed a datacube down on the medical tray and tapped the top, activating the built in holoprojector.

Most High A'armo'o's face appeared. It was covered in sweat, his hair was matted and wet, his eyes were red with exhaustion.

"I know you are tired, men," he said. "You may be feeling that we are throwing our lives away for nothing, but nothing could be further from the truth than that feeling of despair," A'armo'o said.

I looked up and Great Grand Most High of Armor A'armo'o motioned to the cube, bringing my attention to it.

"If they get past us, get into the city at our back, then every-thing Gunner Ha'almo'or has done is for naught! The lemurs are coming with fire and wrath and I am confident they will join our fight against these terrible machines for, like us, they are the liv-ing! Every hour, every minute, we hold, is another child, another man, another woman, that Ha'almo'or can rescue and seal away in the shelters he has created and defended with nobody but mechanics and clerks armed with whatever castoffs he could scavenge!"

His volume rose even higher.

"For all of your careers you have done things, followed orders, that you wondered if they were honorable! Now you know why you are wrapped in battlesteel! THIS, this moment RIGHT HERE, is why you were born," he bellowed out. "Fight, and gouge one more minute from the Precursors cold metal claws for Gunner Ha'almo'or and his loyal troops! Give him the time to rescue one more colt, one more calf, one more filly! Buy him that time, and you will not die in vain! I will be by your side and together we will form a bulwark between the Precursors and those Gunner Ha'almo'or fights to save even if we must do so with our destroyed tanks and our stacked dead bodies.!"

The cube winked out and I found myself crying.

"That speech rallied my men, enabled us to push them back from the cities," he said. "I lost ten thousand tanks, each full of the finest Lanaktallan to ever trot across tarmac, but we pushed them back."

He was silent for a moment, staring at me.

"I am proud to call you brother, Gunner Ha'almo'or," he said softly. "I must return to my tank. The battle still rages on, despite the addition of the Terran's might it is still in doubt."

I nodded, still weeping. He moved to the door, then paused. "Someday, I hope, you can look back at these dark days with pride."

And he was gone.

I sat for a long moment after the doctor and Matron left. Eventually I wiped my eyes and looked at Mal-Kar. "Help me out of the sling."

He didn't question, didn't protest, just helped me untangle myself from the medical instruments and the sling. He let me lean on him for a moment as the anesthetic beam and nanites suddenly cut off and my leg began to ache.

I dressed slowly, putting on my vest, sash, and flank covering, then peeked out the flap of the fabric 'walls' that made up my little recovery area.

Just the wounded.

So many of them.

I trotted out, head held up high, acting as if I had no business within the recovery tent. When we exited I exhaled in relief.

My first breath of the outside air carried the bitter tang and metallic taste of the last several days.

Mal-Kar followed me as I moved through the tents that had gone up while I had been asleep, following me as we headed for where the vehicle were. Terrans ran every which way, sometimes calling out to one another, many of them carrying objects or dragging cables as they worked.

My tank sat on the tarmac, in a parking space, surrounded by other tanks.

I had gotten eight steps when a Fifth Most High Tank Commander confronted me.

"Where is your tank, trooper?" he asked me, his tendrils limp and exhausted. "We return to battle soon, the Precursors are massing for another assault in hopes of pulling the Terrans away from the manufacturing machines."

"There, Most High," I said, pointing at my tank.

He looked it over with his side eyes, still keeping me in his vision. I could see my tank, knew he could see it as clearly as me.

"GREAT HERD EMERGENCY SERVICES" was spray painted on the side in blue paint. The armor was patched with beaded welds. The barrel was discolored from being fired so often. The hoverskirts were patched, the plasma guns replaced by Terran kinetic weapons.

"Identify yourself," he ordered.

"Gunnery Assistant Fifteenth Class Ha'almo'or," I said, drawing myself up and saluting.

He stared at me for a long time, something I didn't recognize passing through his eyes. He moved aside, making a motion with his hands for me to continue on toward my tank. I got five steps away when he called out my name. Not my rank, just my name. I stopped, turning to look at him.

"My mother was among those you have saved, Gunner Ha'almo'or," he said slowly. "I will never forget that you saved her despite the way the Great Herd dishonored you."

"You, and her, are welcome, Most High," I said.

Karelesh waved from where they were sitting on the cupola of the tank, chewing on a ration bar. I nodded, moving up and pressing the touch-plate to lower the back deck.

"Round up your crew, alert the grav lifter crews and the bus crews," I said.

Mal-Kar nodded and jogged away.

"We going back out?" Lu'ucilu'u asked from her place at the EW console when I clattered in, my cast thumping on the deck.

"The Precursors are intending on attacking the city again," I told her.

Karelesh dropped inside the tank, still chewing on his ration bar. His hands quickly went over the controls and I felt the tank start to vibrate as the fans spun up to speed.

I put my face to the sight and toggled the power. I was carrying XM-3821 plasma cannon rounds, the two letters letting me know I was carrying Terran ordnance. The status came back at 87% after I triggered a burst of air through the chamber to clear the debris.

After a few minutes Feelmeenta let me know the others were ready to go.

Eight other tanks would be joining us, as would two platoons of Terran Light Powered Infantry and a squad of Telkan Marine Infantry. Feelmeenta let me know that we had air support and artillery support, via the Terrans, should we need it.

It made me feel better as we moved back into the burning city. The thick smoke blocked normal vision, even created interference for the tank's sensors.

It didn't block out the wailing that could be heard even through the thick armor of the tank.

Undeterred, we drove into the city anyway, the Goodboi's and Simbas bounding along beside us.

There were more to save.

PAIN

The sound of the cutting bars was loud, the city hushed even as it wailed in pain. Each time the powered cutting bars (Mark II) ripped through the tree rapidly, felling it. Mal-Kar and Karelesh used cutting bars given to them by a Terran to cut the trees into smaller lengths. Lu'ucilu'u and I used stick-on graviton lifters and a tractor-pressor beam to move the logs to the sides of my tank, the sides of the two buses, the sides of the combat grav-lifters. There other members of my work crew tied them to the sides with heavy cargo straps.

Several of the civilians manning "Refit Point Delta" were filling sandbags, working tirelessly to shovel dirt into sacks that they tied off and stacked. The sandbags were passed from person to person in a living chain, to be put upon the vehicles as one more layer of armor. They were stacked on the sides of grav-lifters, my tank, and secured with endosteel cargo netting. They were layered two layers thick inside the hoverbuses, with panels of endosteel plating in between the two layers.

Which was why both buses had Terran grav-lifters welded to the side to help lift the massive public transports.

A white flash made everything go flat seeming as the shadows vanished. The rumble came next, the shockwave moving the trees back and forth.

ATOMIC ATOMIC ATOMIC flashed in my vision right before another white flash lit the sky.

The civilians and what few military I had with me ignored it, continuing their work.

A N'Kar who had been a servant for a Most High was half out from under hover-fan three's skirt. Cables went from the power plugin on a nearby grav-lifter and vanished under my tank, allowing the N'Kar to weld a patch to the hoverfan skirt to fix a hole blown in it by Precursor fire.

I leaned forward and rested my head against the battlesteel of my tank, closing my eyes and feeling exhaustion fill me.

I had been awake for twenty hours since I had left the medical clinic and led my men into the burning city again.

Twenty more hours in the burning hellscape that had been a living city.

Five thousand people sealed into the bunkers even as they cried out to me to not entomb them below the earth.

But so many dead were sprawled in the streets, half-visible from collapsed buildings, or reduced to a smear on the wall.

You cannot save them all, Ha'almo'or, the matron's voice came back to me.

No, but I can try, I told her in my mind.

"Most High, eat," Feelmeenta urged me, tugging on my lower right arm.

"I am not hungry," I told her.

It was true. I was too exhausted to feel hunger any more.

"Eat," my electronic warfare specialist ordered. She held up a ration bar. "Eat, or I'll tell the Terrans you have been awake for twice as long as you should have been as well as the fact you escaped from the hospital."

I sighed, taking the ration bar and peeling the plas off of it. It wasn't Great Herd standard. The wrapper was brown, with a picture of a smiling Lanaktallan matron on the wrapper and the words "Goody Yum Yum Bar" on the side.

The Matron was in charge of making sure that the colts, fillies, calves, and wounded were all seen to. A Terran had asked her to smile real quick and then her image had appeared on the package the next time I had been handed a ration bar.

I'd seen the Terrans of the Sustainment Battalion pull them out of their fabulous nanoforges by the box, each box containing thousands of bars.

The bar was good. Rough coarse grain seed and dough, some kind of sweet and chewy center. It filled my first stomach, easing the dull pain, and I felt energy return to my body.

"Do we have any targets or is it another sweep?" I asked, taking another bar and opening it.

This one tasted of berries, was white with a center of sweet and thick crumbly dough.

It was the best thing I had ever tasted.

"Another sweep," Feelmeenta told me. She held up a canteen and I gratefully took it, drinking deep, enjoying the slight tart citrus flavor.

It was such little things, that the Terrans did and we were emulating, that made life bearable.

ATOMIC ATOMIC ATOMIC

I hardly noticed the flash, the rumble, of the gentle push of the shockwave that made the treetop sway.

Two civilians I did not know exited the interior of my tank. The waste reclamation system had failed, leaving the crew compartment thick with dung on the floor. I had helped scoop it out with sheets of plas during the day.

When we had arrived the two civilians, both Telkan, had gone in with pressure washers.

The N'Kar slid out from under the hoverfan, nervously rubbing his skin. "It should hold, Most High," he said. His voice was soft and submissive, like all of his people, but I could see the determination to do a job well done in his eyes.

"I thank you," I told him. "Once we leave will you be going to the shelters?"

He shook his head. "No. We will stay. We have guns now, given to us by the Terrans, as well as battlescreen projectors to protect this place. We will stay here, in case you need us."

The makeshift ambulance nosed its way into the clearing, settling down with the snarl of badly tuned graviton lifters. The back lowered and the filly from the first day clopped down. Gone was the uncertainty of youth, she moved with her head high, one hand on her medical bag, and she surveyed the area like a lord of old.

Two Goodbois and a Simba moved with her, the Goodbois on either side and the Simba behind her. All of them had the holographic light to make them look furry and somewhat harmless.

I had seen the twin linked rapid fire autocannons on the back of a Simba rip apart a Precursor war machine ten times the Simba's side with less than three seconds of fire. I had seen a Goodboi fire missiles at a Precursor air striker, knocking it out of the sky in a greasy explosion and rain of burnt and blackened metal, seen them fire the heavy tribarrel that had risen out of their back to destroy Precursor machines.

I had also seen them search out survivors in a collapsed building.

Like all things Terran, looks were deceiving.

When she saw me she trotted up to me even as I unwrapped another Goody Yum Yum bar.

"You will hold still, Most High," she said. Her voice was raspy, the voice of an older Matron, and her old eyes were red from exhaustion, but still her eyes and voice were steady.

"As you wish," I told her.

She ran the scanner over my lower abdomen and where my upper torso joined my lower body.

"Your heart is in good condition. The cyberware reports no cardiac events," she said, drawing up. "Your bloodwork looks good and your vitals are excellent once exhaustion and combat has been accounted for. How are the eyes?"

"Good. I am used to them now," I told her.

"And your foot?" she asked, pointing at the cybernetic replacement for my hoof.

"Still slightly heavy to my senses," I said.

She nodded slowly. "That it to be expected. You are cleared for duty, Most High Ha'almo'or."

"I thank you," I told her.

"Ambulance One is ready to deploy with you," she said. She trotted around to face the makeshift ambulance with "GREAT HERD EMERGENCY MEDICAL SERVICES" painted on the side with blue paint stick. She turned at the waist to look at me. "Do not attempt to argue with me, Most High."

"I welcome your efforts," I told her.

She could feel my sincerity and nodded. A nod of a Matron far older then the teenager I had seen on the first day crying over the dead.

She trotted back to the makeshift ambulance, the Goodbois and the Simba following her.

Again, the warning, followed by a rapid fire series of detonations.

The Terrans were, to use their own words, 'giving the clankers Hell' out there, pushing them back step by bloody step from the cities even as they sent into the cities their power armor infantry and tanks in with Most High A'armo'o's tanks in order to clear out the Precursor Autonomous War Machines.

"Your tank's ready," the two Telkan said. They were wearing plastic coveralls over heavy laborer coveralls to keep from getting wet.

"Thank you, both," I told them.

The two Telkan made motions of embarrassment before they shuffled off, carrying their power washer and the water tanks with them.

I clopped up the ramp, settling into the combat couch. I leaned forward and pushed my face against the gunner's sight. I activated the tank's systems and felt it come to life around me as my faithful crew climbed in, the power ramp whining as it raised, the load of sandbags attached to the outside face providing more weight than the motors were used to.

I ignored the smell of burning metal.

Mal-Kar drove the tank out of the spot in the woods, weaving between the camo nets hanging between the trees. According to the Terrans they would scatter LIDAR and RADAR and prevent Precursor scanners from spotting anyone in the woods.

We passed holes dug in the ground by determined civilians armed only with shovels. Inside each hole were three or four civilians behind a heavy gun.

There had been plenty that had never been fired and only dropped once for me to arm them with.

As we got further out of the forest/park we saw how the holes had cover. Plas covered with dirt, with firing slits. I could see what I had learned were 'ranging stakes' further out, to let the gunners know the range of any targets.

More than a few of the civilians raised a clench fist to my tank as I drove by, some even calling out my name or the name of one of my crew.

I knew I would be punished for what I had done the night before.

I had armed the neo-sapients. Given them the guns that my own people, my fellow members of the Great Herd, had dropped in panicked flight. Ordered them to 'dig in', showed them how to fight, given them Terran technical documents for digging combat positions by hand, Terran documents on how to use the radio net.

They had put the time to good use and had been very persistent in learning what I was trying to teach them.

'Jawnconnor Time' the Terrans called it.

Mal-Kar had written the name "Timekeeper" on the barrel of our tank. A joke that made sense to us, but probably to none other.

We exited the trees, the hovertank hitting the thickly polluted river, sending up a spray of water to either side of us. The lifters, hoverbuses, and ambulance all followed, the water brown with a thick layer of rainbow oily effluvia on the top. Charred bodies and debris slowly floated in the current.

I put them out of my mind, despite the way it made my chest hurt.

We headed into a gap in the river retaining wall, moving into a massive culvert, the thin layer of water spraying up around us.

A dozen Precursor strikers roared by overhead, chased by Terran strikers and air mobile hovercraft, the shell casings from the Terran vehicles raining down around us, making chiming noises as they bounced off exposed armor or the ferrocrete of the culvert.

"Eyes wide, fingers on the trigger," I said over the tiny battle tactical net I'd managed to get cobbled together. It wasn't much, had the wrong headers to be tied into the planetary network, but it worked for our small force.

A building groaned to the side and began to collapse in on itself, the floors inside falling first, pulling the outside frame and facing in after it. It gave a steady roar as it fell in a strange candle-like plume of ferrocrete dust and twisted endosteel. The fires inside colored the dust and smoke red as the building finally finished collapsing and sent up a massive cloud of debris.

The dust washed over us, making the battlescreens crackle and snap at the attempted intrusion.

One of the crew served kinetic weapons on top of Bus Two opened up with a quick burst. I tensed, waiting, but no "Contact" came over the radio and I knew that the gunner had seen something suspicious and reconned it by shooting it a few times.

If Mal-Kar's Digital Omnimessiah didn't want us to recon by fire he wouldn't have invented triggers.

"Got a public communicator message coming in," Feelmeenta said, sitting up in her chair and putting one hand to the side of her helmet. "Immature Lanaktallan female, a bunch of others, they've got children and wounded. I'm patching in Ambo-One."

"Do you have a fix on their position?" I asked.

"Storm drain, one of the Tukna'rn ripped the grate off and got them inside. They've been there since the first day," Feelmeenta said.

"All units, eyes out, we've got survivors," I said over the comlink. I got back "yeah", "yes, boss", "OK", "affirmative", and "Sure."

My men weren't much on radio discipline and proper radio procedure, but they were the finest men the universe had ever known as they followed me through the smoke and fire of the murdered city.

Mal-Kar's gentle touch on the tank's controls wove a smooth pattern to the storm drain. There were kinetic and plasma and laser impact scars around the drain and someone had pushed dumpsters in front of it. The dumpster had all been shattered by combat.

The ambulance moved in front of the tunnel and lowered the back deck. I saw the filly exit with her Simba and Goodboi escorts.

I grabbed my weapon and hit the stud on my couch, the hatch opening and the couch raising as I cocked the rifle. It wasn't the plasma rifle I had previously held, I had no idea what had happened to it. Instead it was a brutal and ugly Terran weapon that shaved slivers of metal off of a block to create some weird variable munition.

The Terran who had gave it to me had set it to APDSDE (armor piercing discarding sabot density enhanced) and I had seen no reason to change it back.

"Most High," Feelmeenta started to protest.

"I will not allow her to go somewhere I am loathe to step myself," I snapped. "Eyes out, scanners up. Get a recon drone, two weapon drones, and a commo drone up, try to establish communication with Refugee Point Lima."

By the time I had finished my orders I had reached the tunnel entrance and managed to catch up to the filly, who barely acknowledged my presence as I passed her.

The ferrocrete of the tunnel was pitted and scarred, cratered and scorched, by combat. We passed several PAWM carcasses, their bodies damaged by close quarters fighting.

Some of them looked like they had been attacked with a standard vibro-axe carried by emergency services to get through modern hyper-alloys for rescue missions.

There were bodies of Tukna'rn too. Only three, but each one was a dagger in my chest.

"DON'T COME CLOSER I'LL SHOOT!" was suddenly yelled, the words coming so fast that they nearly blended together. Lights came on, illuminating me and my visor kicked in to compensate for the sudden flood of light.

"Gunner Ha'almo'or, Great Herd Emergency Services, we heard your call," I yelled back.

"Please, our friends need a doctor. They're hurt bad," a filly called out.

"Come up here so I can make sure you aren't a clanker in someone's skin," the voice said. They coughed, a wet sound. "Not falling for that again."

The medic touched my arm and I saw displayed on my visor 'collapsed/punctured lung' as she told me her rough diagnosis.

I turned my visor transparent, moving forward. The Tukna'rn was young, barely adolescent, but he had a discarded plasma tri-barrel in his arms, holding like a weaker species would hold a rifle.

"You're a Lanky," he said, using the slang that had seemed to crop up everywhere.

"I am," I said. "Great Herd Emergency Services. We're here to evac you out."

The Tukna'rn nodded, coughing again.

"You first, it's clear," the filly, no, she was no longer a filly. Fire and blood had washed away her youth. The Matron said.

"If Li'itlewu'un says so," the Tukna'rn protested stubbornly.

I nodded and gestured at the Matron Medic. "Let us go in further."

"They're around the corner," the Tukna'rn said, coughing again.

He moved down the passage, normally used for power, sewer, and water maintenance, around the corner, and stopped.

It was one of the bigger rooms. Maybe used for the depression that would normally be a pool of water, maybe just for maintenance crews to gather. Bedding of wadded cloth were around the wall, ammo boxes obviously picked up from abandoned positions scattered around, and boxes of canned food and liquid nutripaste tanks here and there.

A Lanaktallan filly, not much older than the medic, moved up. She clasped her hands, greeting me.

"I am Li'itlewu'un," she said. "Thanks be that you are here."

I looked around slowly. There a Hamaroosan female sat with a vibro-axe that the handle had been cut in half in her lap. There a Telkan female was drinking nutripaste slurry as she let a N'Kar female tie a bandage on her leg.

All around me was suffering, of civilians who had needed my protection and found me wanting.

The Matron Medic touched her helmet and I heard her give orders for others to come in, to carry litters, to clear one of the buses. I repeated her orders, adding my authority to hers.

"We have a refugee point with shelters," I told the filly. "You cannot stay here. The battle has moved to atomic weapons."

"Will we be safe there?" she asked doubtfully.

"The Terrans have arrived and are pushing the Precursors back, although it is still very fluid right now," I told her. Beyond her the Goodbois and the Simbas deployed purrbois even as the Matron Medic moved through the wounded, putting holotags on them that her assistants could read with their visors.

All too many of them were red for urgent care required.

I watched as the wounded were helped out, heading for the bus. The Matron Medic's assistants were on the bus, letting the two of us know that they were treating as fast as possible.

I put a call across the net for Terran medical assistance. Their medics, their SAR, wore armor that the Great Herd would consider heavy combat armor and carried guns that could shatter a Precursor machine with ease.

Less than a third were remaining when I heard a shout from one of the rear tunnels. Gunfire sounded out, echoing strangely in the tunnels.

"They're coming!" someone, it sounded like an immature Akltak, yelled out.

"GET THEM OUT!" I bellowed, charging down the tunnel, my warsteel hoof shedding sparks as I ran.

The two Akltak females were ducked down behind a barrier as I turned a corner. Beyond them I could see Precursor machines rushing down the tunnel toward us.

The two teenagers were only armed with axes.

"Fall back, retreat to the main chamber and follow your leader out," I ordered, lifting up the rifle.

"But what of you?" one asked.

"I will be fine," I told her.

Either they would kill me, or not. Either way, I could buy precious seconds to get the wounded out.

I hit the firing stud and the magnetic accelerator rifle opened up with a roar. Despite the fact it used magnetic force and not chemical propellant, the weapon still flashed at the barrel, a tongue of flame lighting everything up as if it was using propellant.

The heavy magac rounds ripped into Precursors armor, sending one, then another, then another, crashing to the floor of the tunnel in heap.

"We are hurrying, Most High," the Matron Medic told me. I could hear her breathing heavy. "We're loading onto Bus Two."

"I'm coming, Most High," Mal-Kar radioed.

"Negative, hold position. You have to escort the bus back," I snapped, adjusting my fire and raking another machine. "Get the refugees out, damn you!"

"As you command," Mal-Kar replied. I could tell he was unhappy, but I had no time to be concerned as more PAWM drones pushed forward. The rifle was roaring in my hands as I held the trigger down, bracing the butt against one shoulder and using three hands to stabilize it.

Return fire was lashing out at me. Hitting the barrier I was kneeling behind, bouncing off the tunnel walls, ricocheting off my Terran built armor. A hit between my eyes rang my bell but I kept firing, forcing them back with sustained autofire.

My own rifle would have overheated by now, but the Terran weapon's heat bar stayed stubbornly in the low yellow. I would have been out of ammo, but sixty seconds of sustained fire and I still had over 80% of the ammo block left and three more in pouches on my sash.

"THIS TUNNEL IS CLOSED!" I roared out, aiming low, at their treads, their claws, their feet, their legs. The weapon ripped apart battlesteel like tissue paper, the small machines too lightly armored to withstand the fury of the weapon. "THERE ARE LITTLES BEHIND ME AND YOU SHALL NOT PASS ME TO ATTACK THEM!"

A round hit my chest, making me groan, but I fired back, ripping the arms off of the machine. Their dead were piling up high enough now that they had cover as they advanced, some of them pushing their dead in front of them.

I grabbed a grenade off my sash with my lower right hand, pulled the pin with my lower left hand, and side-armed it down the passage even as I kept firing, the weapon less accurate now that I was only holding it with two hands.

The grenade went off with the bright bluish-white snap of antimatter, showering the tunnel with droplets of molten battlesteel and shrapnel. I felt pain in my right flank but didn't care.

"Almost out, two more loads," the filly, no, the Matron, told me.

"GET THEM OUT, DAMN YOUR EYES!" I shouted at her as I grabbed another grenade. "YOU SHALL NOT PASS BY ME!"

My mouth tasted of hot copper and bitterness as I kept shooting. A round glanced off my visor, cracking it, but I paid no heed as I threw the grenade into their midst. It went off with a sharp crack and a gout of liquefied battlesteel sprayed my foreleg.

I did not care.

In or out of a tank, I was the armored bulwark of the Great Herd. None may pass by me and live.

I was the people's will made manifest.

A sudden urge made me duck right before a hypersonic rocket was fired, streaked over my head, and blew a crater the size of my chest out of the wall behind me, showering me with ferrocrete.

I answered the rocketeer with another burst that found something good.

The robot exploded, the flame and wave of shrapnel washing over me.

"Last trip, Most High!" the Matron yelled. I could barely hear her. I was half deaf, but did not care.

I began backing up, throwing my next to last grenade as I did so. My rear eyes could see the passage was clear and I was easily able to navigate it.

But I had to do it step by step, keeping up the fire, the punishment, the denial on the Precursor machines.

They charged as they came around the tunnel and I answered with my last grenade and more fire from my rifle.

"YOU!" I roared out. I grabbed a vibroaxe that someone had left on a box and threw it overhand, knocking over a robot when the handle hit it. I kept backing up.

"SHALL!" I bellowed, spraying them with full auto fire as I entered the now empty room. I kicked over a box of plasma rounds, scattering them across the floor.

"NOT!" I slung a tank of nutripaste into the middle of the floor and put a burst into it, exploding the pressurized tank so that slurry sprayed out.

"PASS!" The machines rushed into the room as I backed into the tunnel that would lead outside.

"BY!" I backed halfway around the corner and changed my aim.

"ME!" The hypervelocity rounds hit the plasma rounds.

They exploded.

The fire shoved me, the blast wave pushing me down the hallway even though I braced my hooves, sparks showering from my hoofshoes as I leaned forward into the blast. Alarms started wailing and the front of my armor flashed yellow on my HUD, but I did not care.

I kept backing up after the blastwave passed me.

"All loaded, get out of there, Most High," Lu'ucilu'u said.

"Leave the back ramp open!" I yelled, managing to whirl around. I turned backwards at the mid-waist, watching in 'front' of me with my rear eyes, firing the rifle as I galloped wildly down the tunnel. My fire wasn't accurate, but they couldn't dodge and I couldn't miss as I fired 'behind' me.

My tank wobbled into sight, barrel facing backwards, the loading ramp down, the rear battlescreen off. Rounds that got by me sparked off the armor of the tank.

I could see the interior of my faithful tank, Timekeeper*, and galloped up the ramp. I let go of the rifle, letting the autosling pull it tight against my right forward flank as I threw myself against the gunner's sight, lifting my cybernetic hoof.*

The shot lined up, aimed at the scarred and battered chassis of the lead robot.

"YOU!" I stomped the firing bar.

The Terran "Enhanced Lanaktallan Plasma Munition Mark IV" detonated.

The loader whined as I lifted my hoof. The back deck loading ramp was whining as it closed.

"SHALL!" I stomped the bar again. The loading ramp was almost halfway up.

"NOT!" again.

The loading ramp thumped into place.

"PASS!" I fired the final shot as Mal-Kar goosed the fans.

We sped after the convoy as I used my gunner's sight to scan the skies.

"We've got them all, Most High Ha'almo'or," the Matron Medic's rough voice told me. "Nineteenth Evac is landing a dropship medivac at the Refit Point Delta. They're bringing in something called man pads"

"We will go there," I said. I was trembling with exhaustion as I waited for the gunner's couch to move into position. When it did, I collapsed into it, breathing heavy.

I rested my head against the gunner's sight, even as I kept my eyes open and watched. My still biological eyes felt grainy, thick, like slightly abrasive gum was filling them every time I blinked.

Within a half hour we reached the Refit Point and Mal-Kar set the tank down. I kicked the button and the loading ramp whined down as I got up from the gunner's couch. I staggered out, looking at the bus that Terrans were running onto.

I watched as wounded were taken from the bus onto the heavy, brutal looking dropship. It was all black and looked almost unfinished, as if the designers had stopped before doing any cosmetic work and said "Meh, good enough."

Perhaps, to the Terrans, it was aesthetically pleasing.

A Hamaroosan female, barely a teenager, marched up to me,

her hands clenched.

"I bet you think you're some big damn hero," she snarled.

I shook my head. "You needed me days ago and I was not there."

She seemed taken aback for a second, but she clenched her jaw.

"Riding around in your tank like some kind of lord on high while we were fighting and dying in the tunnels," she snarled.

Mal-Kar started to step up, a Hamaroosan female of older years next to him.

"You don't know what you're..." the Hamaroosan woman said.

I held up my hand. "Let her speak."

"Where were you when we needed you?" the teenager yelled. "Where were you when the clankers came?"

I stayed silent. She did not want to hear my words. She needed me, needed the world, to hear her.

To hear her pain.

"Where were you? Where was the vaunted Great Herd?" she screamed at me, rushing forward. Her little fists hit my armored chest as she pounded on me, tears running from her eyes. "Where were you when they killed my sisters and mother and father and little brothers?"

Her knees buckled and she wilted, crumbling to the ground. I knelt down, putting my arms around her. She tried to push me away, crying, weeping, but I held her tight, rocking her side to side.

"I am here now, little one," I told her as I stood up, lifting her. I carried her toward the medical tent. "I am here now and I will not let them harm you as long as I live."

It started raining. Thick, gummy, black rain.

There was a faint flash, a rumble, and the treetops swayed as I pushed into the tent and handed off the girl, who was holding onto me so tight the Matron and the doctor had to pry her arms off of me.

I headed back to my tank, stopping to grab an ammo block to

replace my half used one and eight grenades instead of four.

The tank trembled beneath my hooves as I mounted the loading ramp and clattered to my gunner's couch.

The tank rumbled as we led the way back into the city, the rest of the convoy following me.

There were more who needed me as she had needed me.

GOODY YUM-YUM BARS

"He's trying to get behind us, get on him, Mal-Kar, get on him!" I yelled, my face pressed tight to the worn and flattened foam surrounding my gunner's sight, welding my helmet's visor to it.

"I'm trying," Mal-Kar snarled, his feet moving as he shifted the balance of the fans to slide us to the side harder.

One of the Precursor's companion vessels got a clear shot at us as we slid past a pile of rubble that had been a furniture store. The heavy graser shot caught us a glancing blow, collapsing the starboard battlescreen. The trees we had strapped to the side exploded outward, the violent blast sending burning and charred chunks of wood fountaining into the sky.

But the armor held.

Mal-Kar's maneuvers knocked down several of the smaller units, smaller than a Telkan female, and the tank's weight crushed them. There was some clattering noises as one of them hung up on a fan, but the pitch changed and I knew the fan was still running.

"Almoooost," I crooned, my foot above the firing lever.

Another Precursor machine fired, taking advantage of Feelmeenta rotating up and powering new battlescreen projector cores. The lighter machines, that we were in the middle off, were ripping at us with lasers too weak to do anything more than light up the air between us.

The sandbags that were hit by the heavy laser sagged slightly, pebbles of glass falling from the charred bags, but nothing else. The lasers concentrated on that supposed weakness, but nothing happened.

Mal-Kar found a little bit of speed and my sight slid over the massive Precursor, the size of two double decker buses end to end. The tank rocked as we ran over something slightly larger, bobbling my sight, but it leveled out at just the right time.

"SHOT OUT!" I stomped the lever and the plasma gun roared, heat backwashing into the crew compartment. Even though my Terran made armor I could feel the heat rise.

The plasma shot, the "Enhanced Lanaktallan Plasma Cannon Round Mark IV", hit square where the two articulated body sections met. The ravening psuedo-matter detonated on the armor, caving it in.

"SHOT OUT!" I fired into the hellish flames of the first shot.

The Precursor machine kept turning, but the weapons stopped firing, the battlescreens collapsed. It began crushing its own smaller brethren.

One of its two companions fired at our back deck, but we were past, the shot streaming past us to hit the dead one even as Mal-Kar spun us in place, dragging the front right nacelle to pull us around faster than we would have normally been able to move.

The one that had just fired came into my sights just as the third, fired again. The cupola rang, but the armor held.

"SHOT OUT!" I stomped the bar and the Precursor fired.

Our forward battlescreen collapsed. The wood on the front of the tank exploded, blinding me for a second, but my sight cleared and I stomped the bar again. "SHOT OUT!"

The second one exploded in place as Feelmeenta cried out in victory. The battlescreen on the port side spun up even as she rotated up a new set of cores for the forward screen and Mal-Kar slid us forward even as we rotated.

The third one fired at the exact same time as I stomped the bar.

"SHO-" I started, my durachrome hoof stomping down on the bar.

My shot hit it before it could withdraw its missile launchers, the plasma hitting perfectly. The missile bay was suddenly filled with the stuff that makes up stars, even as it started to reload from automated systems.

The Precursor exploded as its missile stores detonated.

Then it was our turn.

The missiles screamed in, almost two thirds of them picked off by our point defense. Twenty got through, impacting against the remaining logs and the sandbags. Burning wood exploded from the front of our tanks, dirt and sand blew out in a cone. The lasers played over the armor, seeking anyplace that the super-conductor layer didn't dissipate heat fast enough. The two heavy mass drivers fired, one ripping off all the sandbags from the top of the cupola and snapping off the TC's weapon. The other hit the forward glacis of the turret square, most of the energy directed away by the slant of the armor.

For the most part, the armor held.

For the most part.

The front panels inside the crew cab exploded. A bright lance went through the crew compartment and Feelmeenta screamed. Mal-Kar cried out to his digital savior. I cried out in pain and terror. Lu'ucilu'u screamed from her EW panel as it exploded in her face. Karelesh howled in agony. Shrapenl scythed through the cab panels exploded, screens imploded, and part of the armor detonated into the cab. Flames roared up around us even as I heard two fans go dead. The internal fire suppression system went off, filling the cab with inert noble gas in a sudden rush even as the ventilation system suddenly cut off.

The hull rang on the port side as munitions got through the battlescreen and impacted against the wood and sandbags, but the inner lining held.

Mal-Kar kept us moving, cursing, snarling, biting off the words savagery as he steered us.

"Cycling up projectors," Feelmeenta gagged.

I could see dull red light of the burning city streaming through the hole in the cupola big enough for a Telkan to crawl through.

The last one slid into sight.

"SHOT OUT!" I yelled, and stamped the bar.

All I got back was beeping, barely audible over the wailing alarms.

The gun was empty.

A look showed me that there were still twenty-two rounds in the ammo locker.

I stomped the loading pedal.

It beeped back.

The Precursor fired again, the missiles slicing out. Point defense got all but two and those exploded against the battlescreen that had just started to spin up. I changed my grip, grabbing the controls for the coax, opening fire with the Terran 20mm autocannon.

The whole cab was full of smoke and white mist, but a glance showed me that the majority of my crew's vitals were yellow and green.

Karelesh's was flashing red.

Not X'd out.

Just flashing red.

I filed away the data as I hammered the Precursor vehicle with heavy kinetic rounds so favored by the Terran Confederacy. Another shot hit and the hull next to me suddenly acquired a slide down it a good half meter wide and two meters long.

My suit's medical alarms started wailing.

"HERE COMES THE RAIN!" Feelmeenta yelled out over our datalinks. The tank's commo system was dead.

Karelesh regained consciousness, shaking his head. He slapped the controls and the hatch for his gunner's assistant seat popped open. He grabbed the bag of antimatter grenades from the floor where they thankfully still sat undetonated as the seat rose up.

"Transponder squawking!" Lu'ucilu'u called out from the EW station.

The tank was showering sparks, the ass end dragging as I kept up the fire from the coax. The Terran rounds were shredding the armor, blowing huge craters in it, ripping it away.

To reveal more armor.

"Back, pull back," Karelesh coughed as his seat lifted him high enough to grab one of the secondary guns. It was dead, local control only, the computer linkage cut.

Mal-Kar threw the tank in reverse, ignoring that the hover-skirts of the rear plenum chambers folded back and shredded even as he applied full power to lift us up far enough to move.

Computer guided terminal guidance artillery rounds began raining down, hitting the smaller machines that my tank had been able to ignore. Huge fountains of alloys, ceracrete, ferrocrete, dirt, and burning rubble fountained into the air as the thermo-baric rounds detonated.

Karelesh reached into the bag with both hands, did some-thing, then slung the bag overhand, at the Precursor vehicle.

It landed between us even as I raked its forward sensors.

Karelesh grabbed the handle of the hatch, yanking it down after him as he dropped into the tank.

One of the return shots hit the hatch before it got closed, snatching it from his hand, hitting the twisted and wrecked mis-sile pod and blowing it apart.

Shrapnel howled through the cab, clanking off metal.

Karelesh fell to the floor, limp, his icon burning a steady red.

But no X.

The Precursor machine rushed forward, through the falling artillery shells that were detonation around us, the terminal guid-ance systems IDing our transponder and steering the rounds away from us. Feelmeenta gave another cry of victory and I saw our forward battlescreen spin up as I kept raking the forward glacis of the precursor machine as it rushed us even as Mal-Kar sped us backwards.

The grenades detonated under the Precursor machine, breaking it in half, the white flare of antimatter snapping out again and again as they went off beneath the weakest point of the armor.

Mal-Kar dropped the tank onto the ground and Feelmeenta ramped up the battlescreens. We turtled up in the artillery rain, the battlescreens snarling from the blooms of plasma, the shockwaves of superheated air, and the shrapnel.

But the battlescreens held.

I coughed and looked around.

The tank was finished.

Feelmeenta had the medical kit opened and she unbuckled from the seat, half falling, kneeling next to Karelesh. She ran the scanner over him and started pulling out syringes based on the color coding and markings.

Lu'ucilu'u pinged me and I opened the channel.

"Got a SAR team coming in. My board is all over me. I'm injured, Most High," she said.

"How badly?" I asked her.

"I fear I may have to wipe my ass with a hook," she said, bitter humor in her voice.

"Do so gingerly," I advised.

She snorted as I changed the channels. "Mal-Kar, status?"

"The tank is..." he started.

"To the Digital Garbage Pile with the tank. What is your status?" I snapped.

"Hard to breathe, but the suit's medical kit is keeping me from being in pain," he said.

"No missing limbs? No missing tail? All of your eyes there?" I asked.

"No, Most High. My suit is telling me I have broken chest rings, that is all," he said.

"Relax, Mal-Kar. I do not believe our tank will be going anywhere," I told him.

The datalink pinged as I switched.

"Feelmeenta, how is he?" I asked.

"Bad. He's stable right now, thank the Digital Omnimessiah for the Terran medical kits that the Matron insisted we take," Feelmeenta said. "He lost a hand and part of his forearm, internal injuries. His armor held though."

"And you?" I asked.

"I will miss my tail," she said softly.

"Very well. SAR is on the way," I told them. I clicked through channels until I got to the recovery vehicle. "Vul'Krit, this is Ha'almo'or, do you read? Over."

"I read you, Most High," the N'Karooan said. "We're on our way, a half mile out if your transponder is still attached to your tank."

I chuckled. "I believe it is. Ha'almo'or, out."

We sat in the dark tank as the breeze moved through it. The black rain dripped in through the gaps and there was a faint flash followed by a rumble.

I heard impacts on the ground and there came a knocking at the hull.

"13th Evac SAR," came the loudspeaker projected voice.

"We are here," I called back. "We have wounded. One badly."

"The loading ramp's jammed, we'll have to pry it open," the speaker said.

"I do not think it will matter much in the grand scheme of things," I told the speaker.

Heavy gauntlets pushed through the gap, the battlesteel flexing and bending away. The hands pulled open the back loading deck, where it fell to the ground with a crash.

The logs covering it were smoking from a hit we'd taken and not even realized.

The armors looked fearsome, despite the fact they were silver.

They took Mal-Kar and Karelesh first, hurrying them out on grav-stretchers. I watched as they loaded Feelmeenta and Lu'ucilu'u onto stretchers and carried them out.

One of the armored medics knelt down next to me, looking me over.

"Are you just trapped or is your armor breached?" He asked, playing a white light over the anti-spalling liner that had curled over my rear legs.

"Trapped, I believe," I told him. "I have been holding still and trying not to give into panic."

The face shield nodded. "All right. Let's cut this away."

I held still while the heavy fusion torch built into the medic's armor cut away the liner. It fell to the floor and the pressure over my rear legs eased.

"Don't move yet," the medic told me. He scanned me again. There was a beep and he put his scanner down where my abdomen met my lower torso. "No cardiac events. Your heart was beating pretty hard, but that's to be expected in combat."

He shook his head. "You should still be in recovery, with how recent that cardiac cybernetic implant is."

"This is the duty I must perform," I said stiffly.

"I getcha. All right, let's get you out of here," he said. He cut through the jammed arm rests and helped me out of the seat. I trotted down the ramp just as the recovery vehicle pushed its way through the wreckage, backing up. Vul'Krit was half out of the driver's hatch, waving at me, as he slowly came to a stop.

The medivac striker lifted off, my loyal crew out of the fight, and I sat down on the ramp. I popped open my face shield and slowly unwrapped a Goody Yum Yum Bar, the Matron smiling at me. There was a joke printed on the inside of the wrapper.

One cannibal looks at the other and says "Does this comedian taste funny?"

The crude, horrific joke made me bray out laughter as I sat on the loading ramp, surrounded by destroyed Precursor machines. Vul-Krit moved up to me and patted my shoulder.

"How are you holding up, Most High?" He asked me.

"Much better now," I said, holding up the bar. The sweet doughy outside was delicious, and the berry gelatin interior was crisp tasting and delicious.

"Those bars are the best," he agreed. He waved his hands. "All right, crew, let's hook up the Most High's tank!"

Three hulking Tukna'rn adults exited the vehicle, two grabbing the heavy cables and pulling them along. The third carried heavy graviton lifters over to magnetically attach them to my tank.

"These guys were maintenance workers at one of the factories. I kinda told them they work for me now," the N'Karooan rubbed the top of his head where short fur was growing in. "I needed crewmen."

"I approve," I told him. I took another bite and held it in my mouth, touching it with my feeding tendrils, absorbing the taste and texture. I closed my eyes, even my two cybereyes, and relished the sensation.

"Hooked up, boss," the Tukna'rn said, slapping his hands together. I opened my eyes and saw that another one was bringing over a pack of brown bottles that I recognized as narcobrew. Vul'Krit grabbed one, opened it, handed it to me, then grabbed one for himself. The three Tukna'rn each grabbed a bottle, cracking them open with the sharp fizz of good quality narcobrew.

We sat on the back deck, drinking the thick beer, as strikers roared by overhead. Four times there was the faint flash of far away atomic blasts.

"Those Terrans can fight, boss," one of the Tukna'rn rumbled. "Never seen anyone got at the Precursors like that."

Vul'Krit nodded. "Dam crazy lemurs, but they make good food bars and narcobrew."

We fell back to silence until the narcobrews were done.

"I think I will sit on my tank," I said.

"Sure thing, boss. Be about an hour drive back anyway," Vul'Krit said. He tossed me the last narcobrew. "Drink up, boss."

I climbed clumsily around to the front of my tank, my cybernetic hoof clunking on the damaged battlesteel. I sat down and cracked open the bottle, staring at the wreckage around me as Vul'Krit began towing my tank back to the base.

Time flowed by slowly and I avoided thinking by staring at the surroundings but actually looking at nothing. I finished the narcobrew and threw the bottle into the ruins, seeing it bounce twice before shattering.

I opened up another Goody Yum Yum Bar.

Why can't you trust atoms? They make up everything.

That got another braying laugh from me.

We were moving through a section of the city that I had

cleared days before, the habs all collapsed, when I spotted her.

She ran out into the street, waving a cloth, stumbling and almost falling as she chased after us.

"Vul'Krit, stop the vehicle," I ordered, standing up. I jumped down, almost collapsing from the shock of jumping from such a hieght, and trotted up to her.

I held my rifle in my hands and watched around myself with all six eyes.

"Please, help us! She can't move any more and won't wake up," the little immature female Cemtrary cried out as I got close. "She's too heavy for us to move!"

I could see her fur was singed and blood stained. She had bandages and what looked like medical gel on her in patches.

"Please, Overseer, help us," she cried out.

"Lead me to 'her', little one," I ordered.

"We covered her up with the hood of a car," she told me.

I kept close watch around us. I would not be fooled. There was the wreckage of many Precursor infantry robots around, even three of the heavier combat machines burning nearby.

It looked like they had put the hood of a vehicle over the top part of a robot. Massively thick legs stuck out from under the hood. Powerful hands, one holding a heavy thick stubber with a bird of prey done up in burning gold on the side. Around the covered prone figure were two dozen Cemtrary females, most of them holding tiny versions of themselves.

I grabbed the hood and threw it to the side.

Her face was severe, pale, I could see her skull where three heavy divots had blown bone out in a crater. I could not see her brain, but the divots blown out of her skull probably did not mean anything good for her. She had long flowing blonde hair. Her eyes were closed, blue around the corners of her mouth and nose, but she was still breathing heavily. Blood was running from her nose.

"We can't pull her, Overseer, she's too heavy," one of the Cemtrary girls said.

It was a Terran over three meters tall, entirely clad in heavy thick plates of armor. There was a bird of prey on the chest, just as it was on the weapon, the warsteel smoldering white in silent fury. She had a torch on each shoulder, the torches smoldering, and what looked like some kind of ejector system on her hip.

"I'll bet she is," I said softly. I turned on my datalink. "Vul'Krit, get a grav-dolly and a power lifter. We've got a Terran heavy power armor troop down and unconscious."

"All right, boss," Vul'Krit answered.

I knelt down, staring at the Terran. She was beautiful, in a coldly angry kind of way. She faintly smelled of incense and scorched warsteel.

The two Tukna'rn came through rubble, pulling the grav-dolly with the power-lifter on one end.

"What is that?" one of them asked.

"It's a SHE, not a WHAT," one of the Cemtrary snapped.

"Yeah," one of the smaller ones holding tight to her back added.

"A Terran," I said.

"Huh. OK, boss," one said.

"Be careful with her," another Cemtrary female added.

They carefully moved her onto the dolly. She was too heavy for the two muscular Tukna'rn to move by themselves, so they used the lifter system. I glanced at the gauge and saw that she weighed just over two tons.

"Follow me," I ordered. I pushed the grav-dolly myself, my prosthetic hoof striking sparks as I walked.

"What happened to your foot, Overseer?" one asked.

"Precursor blew it off," I told her. "I am no-one's Overseer. Call me Ha'almo'or, little one."

"Oh," she said.

I watched as the little ones climbed into the recovery vehicle, then took a hooked chain and attached the grav-dolly to my tank so we could tow the wounded Terran. One of the Tukna'rn came around to help me and hand me another nacrobrew.

I sat back on the front armor, took out another Goody Yum Yum bar and began to eat, sipping at the narcobrew as I read the wrapper.

Why was the burglar so emotional? He took things personally.

I brayed laughter as the black rain fell around me.

CHOICES

Ten Thousand bleed before me
Ten Thousand cry behind me
A Thousand stand beside me
War has destroyed us

The Hikkenite female's voice was soft and pure, wafting through the refit point. It merged with the howl of the cutting bars hacking down trees, the grinders working on vehicles, the shouts of the Terrans as they worked, and the sound of the ad-hoc crews doing what they could.

War has changed us
War has united us
Once he stood alone, called a cheat
Now we stand as one among many

Beside her an immature Welkret female was playing a slow melancholy tune to go with the Hikkenite's singing. She had a little wind instrument, the end against her mouth, the reed parallel to her face. Her fingers worked as played, strong fingers that I had seen holding down a Terran with a blown off arm as the medics worked on him.

A Herd of a thousand voices
Feral, primitive, Lanaktallan united
We stand with one purpose
To protect those that cannot fight

I sat in the mud, my legs folded underneath me, leaning over slightly to rest my shoulder against the expended missile pods. I felt exhausted, like I had been up since the dawn of time. I checked my chono in my helmet and saw I'd been awake for nearly thirty-eight hours. Over twice the recommended time for even sleep deprivation training.

Podling, Colt, Filly, it no longer matters
Every voice lost is one too far
Every inch gained is a thousand short
Every machine destroyed is a million too few

My biological eyes closed and I was loathe to open them. The two cybereyes let me see anyway, almost with perfect clarity.

I thought about how an old Lanaktallan on the sixty-third floor of the hab-complex I had grown up in had cybereyes and often complained that he could not see things clearly, only shapes and shadows and a slight bit of color.

My eyes felt like they were stuck together when I opened them again at a crash.

Yet we stand
We stand filled with rage
With loss
With the conviction that no more shall die

Another tank had been pulled in by the recovery vehicle and I knew I should get up, go over to it, but I couldn't seem to find the strength of stand up as I listened to the beautiful voice of the young girl singing such a melancholy song.

I saw a Telkan that I recognized from the first days, a Telkan that I had seen bring his family and watch me seal them away in the first shelter. He left where he was eating, shoving the rest of his Goody Yum Yum Bar in his mouth as he pulled a paint stick from his pocket.

Boot, Hoof, Talon, or Fin
Fist, Claw, Gauntlet, Blade
Nothing matters more than the lives behind us

I closed my eyes slowly, my cybereyes still watching the doctors working behind the cloth. I could see the two inch thick plates of armor that had been pulled off the Terran woman, hear the beeping of machinery.

Four times an arc of bright red blood has sprayed across the cloth, arterial spray as the doctor's struggled to save her life.

I could see the monitor where six lines moved steadily. A device to measure brain activity that I knew was connected to the fallen Terran who had led the foundlings out of the ruins, fighting alone, protecting them, calling out her faith to the Digital Omnimessiah to give her the strength to save them.

Skies burn
Innocents scream
Metal screeches
Rounds explode
The singer's voice was low, soft, as she sang the dirge.

Only one line of the brainscan had a single blip. Every few seconds it would give a little hiccup.

Only one.

I wondered if she was in pain.

I hoped not.

We we will survive
Not Confederacy, not Herd, not Hive or Pod
Our hearts, our peoples
We die so they can live
Into my vision walked three Terran females. Huge, covered in heavy armor, the torches mounted to their armor so they rose up over either soldier burning with a bluish-green flame. The bird of prey on their chests burning harsh white. They moved with the slow looking over-exaggerated movements of someone long used to power armor.

They went by me and into the tent. I could see them move to where the doctor was working. Hear the Matron protest and the doctor snap at them.

They can laugh and play
While we toil away
With gun and grenade
Blade and Hoof
One came out, moving toward me. I struggled to get up, failed, and tried again, my joints aching, my muscles unresponsive. I managed to get all the way up, my legs shaking like a new-

born colt, but my back straight and my chin lifted as I looked at them with my visor clear.

"You are Most High Ha'almo'or?" one asked.

I nodded. "Nearly," I told her. "What is left of me."

"I am Sister Tiffany Dargetta, the Sisters of Wrath, fighting for the Dark Crusade of Light beneath the hand of the Immortal Osiris of the Warsteel Flame and Joan Mentissa," she said.

"I am Assistant Gunner Fifteenth Class Ha'almo'or, of the Great Herd," I told her.

"You have saved our sister from shame. Completed her mission after she fell to her foes," Sister Dargetta said. Her voice was stern, but held a hint of pain I could hear. "However, our sister now faces a choice she cannot make."

I nodded slowly. She motioned to me and I followed.

"Her head wound is grevious. Not enough to kill her, not now, not with your medical services treating her," the Joan said. She waited as I stumbled twice.

She did not offer assistance and I did not expect it.

The wind instrument played solo, the chainswords, the pounding of the sledgehammers, the yelling and shouts of the civilians and soldiers all providing a background. It was beautiful.

It had no place here. It was too pure.

"However, she has been grievously injured, and because of this, there are only two paths left to her," the Sister of Wrath told me. "As you are the one who saved her, you shall be the one to decide her path."

We moved into where the doctor was stepping back. He looked as if he did not approve. The other two were dressing the wounded one in her armor. Her chainsword was on her chest, her hands folded over it.

"What are the paths?" I asked, swallowing.

"Death," the Sister of Wrath said. She moved and made a motion. The other one shifted, and I could see the fallen Sister of Wrath's face.

She had whiskers. Short fur on her face. She had feline ears rising out of her dark hair.

"Or a fall from grace," the sister said. "To embrace what it means to be Enraged, to embrace what it means to be Wrath, more than anyone in the universe."

"Choose," they all said, facing me. "Choose her path."

I did not know her. I did not know her culture, her struggles, what she might have wanted.

"Choose, Most High Ha'almo'or," the Sisters said. "Will she die, or do you will her to live? You have saved her, thus you must decide."

For us victory or death
Either is fine
We fight as one
*So they can **live***

"Live."

WITNESS US

The three female Terrans all nodded at my words. Two began attaching the last of the armor, beginning to pray, the other put her hands to either side of her fallen sister's head, on the thick, heavy shoulder pauldrons. I watched as the face began to change, becoming rounder, softer, the fur changing color to white with streaks of pink.

The burning bird of prey on her chest slowly faded and went out.

I felt a cold wind go through the tent, with a faint moan of suffering.

It was strange. I was not a religious being. I had not begun following the Terran's digital religion. I had no belief in superstition or magic or mythical events.

But standing there, watching, I felt a chill down both of my spines.

The armor, formerly white with red markings, began to change colors. Pink and white, smeared in a strange amateurish way. The woman's face began to look more youthful, more innocent, more childish.

Her lips parted, showing sharp interlocking carnivore teeth had replaced the even white squares of omnivore dentation. She drew in a shuddering breath.

The monitor displaying her neural function gave a hiccup as on line spiked and the others twitched.

"doki" the fallen one whispered.

I don't know why, but I swallowed thickly, feeling a trickle of fear.

I could see her datalink on the side of her head. There was

white and pink enamel crawling across it, covering the black warsteel. It began to look more ornate, gold and silver inlay starting to form on it like frost on a window.

Beep.

'doki'

I watched fur crawl down her arms from her shoulders. White with pink stripes and swirls and blotches. I could see circuitry spreading on and under the flesh right before the soft looking fur covered the pale bloodless flesh. The two sisters covered the fallen one's arms with her armor, locking the heavy plates in place. The white and pink enamel and paint started spreading from the armpit and shoulder, again reminding me of frost spreading on a window.

beep

'doki'

She shifted slightly, the power armor hissing and clattering. I reached out, picking up one hand, and was startled at how light her arm was. I took her hand and placed it on her cutting bar where it rested on her torso, the handle beneath her chin. The Sister of Wrath on the other side lifted her arm, her power armor hissing and her face hardening with effort.

Her hand and arm were as light as a child's as I put her hand on the hilt of her blade, folding them over one another.

beep

'doki'

Shuddering and tremlbing, I picked up the thick plate for her thigh and lifted it into place. The Sister of Wrath beside me lifted the woman's leg by her knee, letting me put the armor beneath her leg. I saw spikes erupt from the armor, long thin barbed spikes.

A part of me didn't want to place the woman's leg into the armor, but I did so anyway.

Fur started moving down from beneath the groin armor. I picked up the front of the leg armor and set it into place, hearing it click and lock into place. I could hear internal systems start to click as I knelt down and picked up the piece to go under her lower leg. I wasn't sure what the Terrans called it. I doubted they called it a fetlock.

"You do her honor, dressing her," Sister Dargetta told me, her hands still on the heavy shoulder plates. "The last suit she shall ever wear."

"It is good that she be clad," I said. I locked her foreleg into the armor.

beep - - - - beep

'doki doki'

I heard another song start but could not hear the worlds, just the melancholy tones of the woodwind and the words.

One of the Sisters handed me her heavy weapon, but it was lighter than I thought it would be. The bird of prey on either side was dark, no longer blazing fire. The weapon was dark, black and dark green, looking heavier, bulkier somehow.

At the Sister's motioned instructions I took one of her hands and carefully wrapped her fingers around the grip.

The pink and white smears and daubs spread from her hand up the weapon. A round circle with eyes and an upturned mouth appeared where the bird of prey had once been.

beep beep beep

'doki doki doki'

The words were still soft, more breathed than spoken, but sounded to me as if they were a lot stronger than they had been initially. There was more spikes in all six of the lines on the monitor that was displaying her neural functions.

I moved around to the other side, putting her armor on her arms and legs with my own two hands.

While I did not believe in magic or superstition, knew that the Terrans used nanotechnology in dangerous ways and that could account for what I was seeing, I still felt as if I was caught up in something I did not quite understand.

The Sisters of Wrath removed the torches from their fallen sister's armor and motioned at me.

"Carry her outside, beneath the sky, so she can hear the voice of her sisters," Sister Dargetta said.

Part of me knew she was too heavy for me, that she weighed

literal tons of armor and dense lemur muscular-skeletal structure.

She was as light as feather in my arms. One hand holding tight to her weapon, the other to the hilt of her cutting bar.

She kept whispering to herself, her lips moving over sharp teeth, as I carried her outside. She should have been too heavy, I should never have been able to carry her.

But she was as light as a feather.

I laid her down on a pallet of expended rocket tubes, stepping back as the clouds seemed to part just enough for a silver ray of sunlight to pierce the clouds and illuminate her face.

The sisters put banners of blank cloth, held up by cruel iron rods, on her back. They replaced the torches, now unlit, on her shoulders. The round smiling emoji on her chest suddenly had hearts replace the eyes, the hearts beating slowly.

"She nears wakefullness," Sister Dargetta said.

"Will she be confused?" I asked.

"She has fallen from grace and is now Enraged, knowing nothing more than Wrath," one of the other sisters said. "She will seek out combat, seek out war, know nothing more than carnage and fury."

I stared at her innocent looking face, now completely covered with fur. "Will she be in pain?"

Sister Dargetta shook her head. "She will dwell in fury and ecstasy, surrounded by beauty and carnage, beyond such things as pain or doubt," she said softly.

"Why is this happening to her?" I asked, watching as her eyelids fluttered. For a moment I could see her eyes. They were feline pupiled, but bright pink, as if she was an albino. Then the eyes seemed to fill with a pink glow and the eyelids closed again.

"She is the fate that awaits all of us, all of the Sisters of Wrath, should we fall from the Digital Omnimessiah's grace and embrace the wrath that fills us all," one said.

"But... why?" I asked.

"She, and we, are bound to Murdered TerraSol," Sister Dargetta said. "Soldiers of the Combine and Imperium, led by Daxin the Unfeeling who became Osiris of the Warsteel Flame, touched and reborn by Vat Grown Luke who became Legion, nurtured and guided by Bellona the Grave Bound Beauty, shown the way of truth and beauty."

The names, although they meant nothing to me, still made my skin crawl as a cold breeze played over my skin despite the Terran armor I wore.

"But our children, the Kawaii Neko Marines, are the youngest of us, the oldest of us, and they await, with open loving arms, all of us who fall from the Digital Omnimessiah's grace," she finished.

doki doki doki

"When she awakens, she will seek out the enemy, consumed with rage, and seek to wipe them from the universe," another sister said.

To the side of me the tank sat silently, "GREAT HERD EMERGENCY SERVICES" written on it with blue paintstick.

"She will be the champion of those without hope consumed with wrath and fury," the other said.

I realized that the Terran female may have been sentenced to a life of horror and I wondered for a moment if I should have just let her die.

"Will she remember who she was? Will she be full of sorrow for what she has lost, what I have consigned her to?" I asked. "Would she have been better off dead?"

They all three looked at one another for a long moment.

"Concern yourself not with such things," Sister Dargetta said. She put her hand on the pink and white hair on top of the fallen one's head. "She will burn with a light of her own."

Her eyes suddenly opened. Bright pink, a low malevolent growl came from her mouth then she smiled wildly. A sweet, innocent, naive smile that made me start to smile back. She struggled to her feet, still smiling, her power armor hissing and whirring. She held her cutting bar in one hand, what I had been told was a heavy magac submachine gun in the other.

The torches on her back erupted in flame, white cored with pink edging. The banners unfurled, showing crude drawings on them.

"Come, sister," Sister Dargetta said, holding out her hand. "Joan Mentissa wishes to bless you."

The furry faced fallen Sister attached her submachine gun to her waist and took Sister Dargetta's hand.

There was a strange fzzzt on my back teeth as all four of the Sisters vanished.

I just stared at where they had been standing, feeling the hair rise up on my spines.

"Most High Ha'almo'or," a voice said.

I focused my attention on my rear eyes, seeing a small Telkan female in white paper clothing waiting patiently for me to see her.

"Yes, little one?" I asked.

She motioned back at the tent. "The Matron wishes to see you. She says it is quite urgent."

"By all means, lead the way," I said. I took two steps and almost went down on my knees, the strength suddenly leaving my body. I stumbled, almost fell, but managed to stay on my feet as I staggered into the medical tent.

The Matron and the doctor were waiting for me.

"Your wounded have been treated, Most High Ha'almo'or," the Matron said, staring at me with a weight of authority that made me want to duck my head in shame. She patted a medical sling. "This sling is for you."

I sighed, allowing the Telkan female to walk me over to the sling and help wrap it around me. The doctor and his assistants removed parts of my armor, stopping when several pieces were stuck to me.

"See you on the other side," the Telkan female said, her face hidden by a sterifield mask.

She pressed a button and darkness took me.

I awoke to the rumbling of atomic weapons shaking the ground. My biological eyes were thick and gummy but my cybernetic eyes were instantly clear and crisp.

A Welkret in a nurse's uniform sat near me, looking at a dataslate. She looked up and smiled. "Welcome back, Most High."

"How..." I swallowed around the thick paste in my mouth. "How long?"

"Nineteen hours," she told me. "You were suffering extreme exhaustion, shrapnel injuries, and second degree burns under your armor."

"My crew," I managed to get out.

She moved over to me, holding a pitcher with straw. I drank deeply, the biting citrus washing away the taste. "Your crew all survived. They will recover."

I hung limp in the sling and breathed a sigh of relief. After a moment I stirred, trying to get my arms and legs to work, but found the anesthetic beam was still in effect.

"Help me out of the sling," I said. "Turn off the beam."

The Welkret shook her head. "The Matron Nurse has stated you are to remain in the sling for the next twenty hours to give your body a chance to heal."

There was the rumble of another atomic detonation that I could feel through the sling.

"There are still people who need me," I told her. I stared at her, blinking with my cybereyes so they made clicking noises. "As you needed me."

The tips of her ears flushed slightly and she looked at me closely. She checked her dataslate, then gave me a once over with a scanner, checking her dataslate again.

"Your hearts look good. Your muscles are responding well to quikheal," she said softly. She looked around, then backed out. After a moment she came back. "We must hurry."

I nodded as she released the anesthetic beam. I clumsily helped her get the sling off me, then had her help me get my Terran armor back on. It was damaged and discolored, but it still fit well.

The Welkret nurse checked for me then motioned. "Go right and out the back of the tent. They're bringing in Terran wounded out front."

"I thank you," I told her.

"Go with grace, Most High," she said softly.

I trotted out, grabbing up a Terran rifle as I did so.

Outside was a whirling chaotic blur of motion, with beings running every which way. I saw two strikers land, one of them smoking, and techs run over to them, one hosing down the smoking one with a fire prevention foam ejector. I realized I had to urinate and followed the sign to where the 'urination station' was located.

I stared in surprise. It was merely pipes sunk into the ground at a high angle, set waist high for the various races. It startled me to see Terrans and other expose their genitals to urinate in the pipes. Still, my body wasn't going to wait much longer as it woke up from the anesthetic, so I trotted over to the line and waited.

It startled me that the Terrans talked to one another in the line. Joking, or asking how one another was holding up, what they were doing. Small talk, as if they were sitting down for a polite lunch, not waiting to urinate in a pipe for everyone to see.

When I got up there I felt somewhat foolish straddling the trough. I looked at the human across from me, a male with dark brown skin, who gave me a Terran smile.

"Straddling the gash slash is the big reason I always reskin as a male for deployments," he told me. "Being able to piss standing up. That's the shit, right there."

I just nodded, unsure of what to say as I let my bladder go.

"Good luck out there, Lanky," he said, buttoning up his fabric pants and moving away. Another took his place, but mercifully didn't say anything.

I finished up and trotted away, feeling somewhat embarrassed by the whole thing.

It only took me a moment to see a tank. It sat off by itself, the armor scarred and pitted. It wasn't my old tank, but it had "GREAT HERD EMERGENCY SERVICES" painted on it with blue paintstick. I trotted over to it, seeing that the loading ramp was down and open.

"Hello?" I asked, moving around to look inside.

A human was kneeling down, looking at the cannon's breach mechanism. He looked up and grinned at me. His face was sweaty and red, his face shield retracted, and his armor had the slight blurring effect of their 'active camouflage' system.

"Specialist Grade Six Lumundaroo," he said, nodding.

"Ha'amo'or," I told him, moving inside. I looked at the interior and noticed it looked a lot different. The breach was heavier, wider, and it looked nothing like any of the main weapons I had trained on. "What kind of gun is that?"

"One-hundred-fifty-five millimeter smoothbore main battle tank gun, right there," he said, patting the breach. "Maximum effective range of seven miles, mission variable munition capability."

"No plasma?" I asked.

He shook his head. "I couldn't fab up plasma gun parts," he admitted. "Your people are running through entire barrels every ten to twelve hours," he shook his head. "No offense, but your wargear is pretty crap."

"None taken," I said. I sat down on the gunner's couch. "How different will this be for me? I am a gunner."

"Superficially, well, you don't have to worry about standoff distance, minimum safe distances, atmospheric attenuation, microprism cloud dispersion, or any of that," he told me. He shifted how he was sitting.

"What about ammunition, I was able to carry seventy-five rounds prior," I said. I flipped the switches so the gunner's sight went live.

He gave a slightly sheepish look. "Well, that's complicated," he said.

I pressed the self-test tab and watched it go through the startup checks. "Explain."

"In the ammunition bay, and now you have two of them, you have a grand total of one hundred rounds. Twenty-five in rapid storage. Seventy-five in the lower storage, which is heavily armored," he said. He shifted again. "I might, and I stress might have gotten authorization to strap a Class-IV nanoforge to this beast, along with a heavy enough mass tank that it can dry-print one round every fifteen seconds or wet-print one every three seconds."

I turned and looked at him. "I welcome such alterations. Anything that will enable me to protect the people of this city."

"This thing has heavier shields, new laminate armor, dual hover-system, replaced reactors. The only thing that's basically the same is the software, and even that's been heavily rebuilt over the last day or so," he told me. "I'm just trying to figure out a problem."

"What problem?" I asked.

He looked at me. "The autoloader isn't working. It doesn't want to work, and I'm not sure why."

"Is the mechanism jammed?" I asked. "Sometimes the rotation cradle's axle can get jammed."

"No," he said. He pulled open the floor plate, exposing the rotation cradle. It acted like the cylinder of a revolver, bringing up ammunition from the ammo hopper. The cradle would extend up as the gun recoiled, loading a round into the chamber as the breach went forward. The cradle would drop back down and rotate, loading a new round into an empty cradle.

He used both hands to shift it back and forth. "It moves, but," he started.

"Most High Ha'almo'or," a young voice said, panting. I turned and looked and saw a young Hikken standing on the loading ramp. He had on a headset and a radio on his hip.

"Yes?" I asked.

"There's a group of survivors in the city. They're pinned down and the Precursors have reentered the city," he told me.

"Do you know how to operate a communications board?" I asked, pointing at the commo station of the tank.

"Yes, Most High, I was a maintenance technician," he said.

"Do you know of any others?" I asked.

He nodded.

"Get them. The tank needs a crew," I said. I turned to the Terran. "If it cannot be repaired, I must go into battle without it. Do the secondary guns still work?"

He nodded slowly. He reached behind him and got a heavy looking tool that I recognized. It was used to manually rotate the cradle. "Secondary guns check out fine," he said slowly. "You know, there's a way to do this."

"How?" I asked. I watched as he moved the metal tool into place, wiggling it to set it.

He slapped the lever for the gun with one hand, the breach rolling back, exposing the empty chamber. The other hand he pushed on the bar, rotating the cylinder. He grabbed the exposed round, slammed it into place, shut the chamber, and then pushed the breach shut.

In less than five seconds total.

"How... how long can you do that?" I asked him.

"Probably longer than this tank will survive," he told me. He gave me a sudden grin. "I've spent all day putting this thing together, I might as well go with you."

"If you wish," I told him. "I would require you to follow my orders."

"I can do that," he said. He chewed his lower lip for a second. "We should probably take two Mantid combat vehicle engineers if that's all right. Maybe even a medic."

I looked around the crew compartment. "Will they all fit?"

He nodded.

"Then I welcome them," I told him. I pulled my helmet off and pressed my face against the gunner's sight. "Hurry. We have little time and the civilians depend on us."

Through the sight I could see the city.

It was still burning.

I touched my implant and heard the filly-Matron answer.

"Gather your ambulance crew, we are needed once again," I told her.

"As you command, Most High," she answered.

I commed the bus crews next, even as my new crew boarded the tank.

The ramp whined as it closed.

--we ride this tank to glory-- one of the Mantids chirped over my implant.

"Victory or death," I said as my new driver rotated the tank, following the instructions of my new navigator.

I pushed my face against the gunner's sight.

"Either is fine."

PLEASE, JUST ONE MORE, PLEASE...

The day was cold as the tank swept through the ruins of the city streets. Down by my right foreleg was a Terran soldier, sitting on a seat that had been ripped out of a bus and welded to the frame so he wasn't thrown around by the maneuvers involved in heavy combat.

I had had my doubts about the Terran soldier operating the loader manually, using a modified socket wrench to rotate the carriage to bring rounds up out of the ammunition bay to a position he could grab them with his hands. From there to the chamber and slamming it shut, he could do the entire thing in less than ten seconds, faster even then the standard autoloader in the tank.

He had operated it for two days, never seeming to slow down or become fatigued.

I had my face pressed against the gunner's sight, looking over the landscape as we moved through the ruins that had been a city housing millions.

"Anything?" I asked.

"No, Most High," my electronic warfare technician, a welkret that had previously worked in the air control tower down by the docks dealing with grav-lifters and hovercraft.

I wrung all four hands. "There has to be more. There has to be."

The Terran touched my shoulder. "Ha'almo'or, we have been sweeping for two hours. Before that, we only found three wounded trapped under wreckage. There are no more."

"Do another sweep, maximum sensitivity," I ordered.

Veltri, the welkret sensor tech, obediently ran another scan. She was scanning for datalinks showing life signs as well as thermal imaging and CO2 plumes.

Nothing.

Jurmek, a shavashan missing part of his tail and sporting a cybernetic eye, swept around a corner where collapsed rubble had completely choked off the intersection but a basement collapse had left enough of a surface for us to move deeper into the city.

Around us skyrakers moaned in pain and exhaled smoke.

"Ha'almo'or, we've swept the city three times, 11th ACR did flyovers, they've got Simbas, Goodbois, and Purrbois, even fishbois out there looking," the human told me. He touched my shoulder again, and strangely enough I could feel it through my armor. "There are no more. I'm sorry."

"There has to be!" I yelled, sweeping the cupola in a full three sixty, looking through my sight.

There was nothing but cold rain, black smoke, and rubble.

And the huddled dead.

"There were millions of beings in this city two weeks ago," I said. I closed my eyes and let my hands drop from the gunner controls. "There were millions."

I straightened up with a jerk. "Do another scan," I ordered. I put my face back against the sight. "Just one more. Please. Just let me save one more."

--adjusting scans-- the little Mantid, who's name involved particle movement deep in a stellar mass but went instead by the number 593, chirped over my comlink.

"Thank you," I told him.

The tank was silent except for the mechanical sounds for a long moment.

"No life signs, Most High," Veltri told me.

"What about the drones?" I asked.

"Nothing," Veltri said.

"We'll do another spiral once we reach the crater in the center of the city," I said. I licked my dry lips, ignoring the slight headache and blurriness even in my cybereyes. "There has to be more. There just has to be. They can't all be dead."

My crew was silent as we slowly moved to the four overlapping craters in the middle of the city, where the Precursor machines had blasted the city when they came in and then when they left as if to mock me.

The rain hissed and crackled against the battlescreens.

Twice I ordered the tank to stop and got out to check in vehicles, check the dead, look under some rubble.

I found nothing but debris and the dead.

As we left the city I pushed myself back from the sight, opening my faceplate so I could rub at my exhausted eyes. My crew stayed silent as I pulled the last stimshot from my satchel and injected it. I grabbed my seat and groaned as my heart started pounding, it felt like my head was going to both explode and collapse at the same time, and all four of my stomachs tried to rebel.

It passed quickly and I felt refreshed, even if there was the taste of zingy metal on my back teeth and my across my feeding tendrils.

I watched around us as we slowly moved out of the city, running a search pattern, looking for any survivor that might have managed to crawl free of their hiding place.

"Again. Head to the city center, we'll spiral out again," I ordered. I pushed my face against the sight. "Please. Please please please."

My crew was silent as we did it again.

When we reached the outside of the city there was the trill of a high priority transmission. Dalpat, a Telkan who used to handle truck dispatch, raised his head up from where he'd fallen asleep on the console. He blinked, touched his helmet, and looked at me.

"It's for you, Most High," he said gently.

"Gunnery Assistant Ha'almo'or here," I said.

"Return to base," the voice said. It was full of authority that hit me in the spinal reflexes.

The transmission cut off.

I moaned and wrung my hands.

Maybe if I just ran one more sweep...

Jurmek turned the tank, heading across the rubble, the smaller stones clattering against the fan blades and nacelle sides. I kept looking, kept searching, trying to spot even the smallest sign of any possible survivors.

I saw none.

I thought about ordering Jurmek to turn around, to do one more sweep.

I just wanted to find one more. Please. Just one more.

But we detected no more lifesigns as we slowly left the city and headed to the base that had grown up around my makeshift shelters. At one point several grav-lifters from the forward operating base joined us as well as the vehicle marked "EMERGENCY MEDICAL SERVICES" in hand written blue paintstick.

We wove between the battle screens and the dirt berms the Terrans and the people who had elected to stay and assist me had created. Tanks were lined up, many of them damaged, and I could see that many members of the Great Herd were waiting in lines as if they were waiting for my damaged and cobbled together tank. There were several Terran tanks present, including a couple of hover tanks.

My datalink clinked as Dalpat messaged me.

"Most High, I'm seeing Great Grand Most High A'armo'o's transponder as well as the transponders for the commanders of Third Armor Division and First Recon Division," the Telkan told me.

"Order the crews to refit their tanks," I said, exhaustion making the order automatic.

"Yes, Most High," Dalpat said, although his voice carried something in it I could not identify.

Jurmek idled the tank into the queue for reloading and refit and bellied it down. After a moment the engines shut off and the back deck lowered down. My gunner's sight retracted into the hull as Veltri stood up from her sensor station.

"We should eat," she said softly.

"Come on, Ha'amo'or," the Terran said. He helped me get the gunner's cradle into position, two of the motors no longer worked right and had to be manually shifted.

"Thirty minutes," I said as I turned around and moved toward the exit.

"As you say, Most High," Jurmek said.

I exited the tank and blinked, the wan sunlight filtering through the clouds bright to my eyes after so long looking through the sight. I stumbled toward where the boxes of Goody Yum Yum bars were sitting, almost tripping twice.

I opened the bar and looked at the joke.

Why did the tree seem suspicious on sunny days? It was a little shady.

I chuckled, a smile breaking through my misery. I moved over and sat down, slowly eating the bar, relishing the taste and washing it down with the G8R8 that the Terran had put in my canteen. My chest hurt and I groaned, leaning forward and closing my eyes, feeling dizzy.

After a moment I straightened up.

And almost screamed in fear when I saw the Matron staring at me with accusing eyes.

"How long have you been awake, Most High?" she asked me.

"Uh," I answered. I stood up slowly, my legs trembling.

"Well?" She asked.

I suddenly remembered something I'd seen a Terran do.

"Look! I'm over there!" I shouted, pointing off to the side where my tank was.

"What?" Frowning in confusion the Matron turned at the waist to look and I galloped away, running behind one of the tents. I hid behind some empty equipment crates, sitting down, and took another bite of my bar, chuckling at my own cleverness.

I opened a second bar.

Why was the archeologist depressed? His life was ruins.

I snorted in laughter and started eating the bar.

"There you are," the Matron filly said. I turned and looked to see she was behind me with two big Terran warborgs. "Don't run away."

I stood up and clattered to the side to get clear of the empty crates, intending on running out the other side of the small passage between the tents.

The Matron stood there with more warborgs.

"Most High Ha'almo'or, what kind of example are you setting?" the Matron asked me.

I sighed and hung my head. She was right.

"Now, how long have you been awake?" she asked me, moving up to me. She tapped my helmet and I saw "MEDICAL OVERRIDE" pop up on the visor right before it retracted.

"Thirty-nine hours," I admitted, swallowing thickly. I had dry mouth again.

She touched the collar of my armor and it retraced. Her fingertips touched my neck as she ran a scanner over my lower abdomen.

"Pupils constricted, rapid breathing, sweaty, cardiac implant is reporting flutters, muscle tremors," she made a chiding noise. "How many stims have you taken?"

"I am unsure," I admitted.

"Please, follow me. You need a medical check," she told me.

"I must return to my duty," I told her.

She put her hand on the side of my face and locked eyes with me.

I suddenly realized how tired she looked.

"Ha'almo'or, there is no-one left in the city. You have gotten them all," she told me. She took one of my hands and slowly led me to the medical tent. "There is nothing left for you to do but allow yourself to undergo medical treatment. The fighting is almost over, so there is no need for you to return to your tank."

"But, there might be survivors under the rubble, too deep for the Terran sensors or the sensors of my tank's drones to see," I protested, following her.

The filly Matron and the warborgs followed me slowly.

She led me into a tent, carefully taking off my armor.

The stench of unwashed hide, scorched hair, and seared flesh as well as the unique smell of old quikheal gel filled my nostrils.

She was quiet as she helped me into the medical sling and turned on the beam.

"Goodnight, Ha'almo'or," she told me.

I struggled against the anesthetic beam.

It pulled me down anyway.

"Can he hear us?" a voice asked.

I was floating in warm water, my eyes closed, my limbs slightly curled. I could faintly hear a thudding heartbeat and the rushing of blood through veins as the water gently rocked.

"Perhaps. He is close to wakefulness," the Matron said. "He is a stubborn male so we are using virtual reality deep level womb simulation to keep his hindbrain relaxed."

"Do not let him leave," the voice said. "He needs to heal. It would be a terrible thing to lose him after all that he is done."

"We won't lose him," the filly Matron said.

"Have you ever seen this before?" the voice asked.

"A few times," another voice said. "Not in one of your people though. Old Iron Feathers is like that."

"It's not uncommon," a third voice said.

"Will he recover?" the Matron asked.

"No. They never do. He will never be the same," the third voice said softly. "He will always wonder if he could have done a little bit more."

I shuddered and relaxed, sinking deeper into the warm water.

The voices receded.

I woke in the treatment tent, jerking slightly and crying out. I was trying to lift a beam that had fallen and blocked a civil defense shelter door in a collapsed building, ignoring the flames around my armor, as Dalpat sprayed a fire extinguisher around me. I could hear the Terran firing his rifle topside, keeping the Precursor light combat robots back.

My eyes opened and it took me a moment to realize where I was.

Mal-Kar sat in a bed opposite of me, slowly eating some type of pudding. When he saw that I was looking at him he smiled and set the bowl down. I noticed he had breathing tubes up his nose and monitors attached to him.

"Welcome back, Most High," he said.

"How are you, Mal-Kar?" I asked.

"Recovering quickly. They say I'll only be in here a day or two more to make sure I don't get fluid buildup in my lungs," he said. "I saw Feelmeenta, they gave her a cybernetic hand."

I nodded.

Mal-Kar looked over and gave a slight wince. "Oh boy, here comes someone mad at you."

The Matron clopped into sight and stared down at me.

"So, are you here or over there, Most High?" she asked, her tendrils curled in amusement.

"I am here," I told her.

"And where will you stay?" she asked me.

"Here," I said.

She put her hands on my shoulders, squeezing gently. "You did all you could do, Ha'almo'or. Do not let what you think should have been eclipse what actually was."

I let me head hang. "I just wanted to save a few more," I admitted softly.

"As did I. It was not to be. The Precursors, they also get a say, and their voice was loud," she said gently. She looked at me. "Rest now. There will be time enough for recriminations later."

It was raining again, but the rain was clear, not longer a black sticky thing, as I limped out of the tent and looked around.

A Terran, possibly the largest I had ever seen, was standing next to a Hikken that was chewing on an empty ration tube. The Terran was talking to a Lanaktallan I recognized and as I trotted across the grass, heading toward my tank, I saw the Terran turn and spit some kind of brown juice.

I had almost made it to my tank when I heard the voice.

"Gunner Ha'almo'or," the voice said.

I recognized it instantly.

Great Grand Most High of Armor A'armo'o.

"Come here, brave one," my commander said.

I nervously trotted over to him, feeling the urge to flee.

"This the one?" the Terran asked, spitting on the ground.

"He is," A'armo'o said.

The Terran turned and looked at me and I noticed he had three stars on his lapel. He looked me up and down for a long moment with his burning glowing red eyes, judging me, weighing me, perhaps seeing more than I thought was there.

"Damn fine job, son. Damn fine," he said. He spit on the ground again. "Took balls."

The Hikken nodded, taking the ration tube out of his mouth. "I am honored to have met you."

Great Grand Most High A'armo'o took my hands in his and stared into my eyes.

"There will be no reprisals against you, Ha'almo'or," he said. He looked around. "Things are changing, in ways you might not understand, but what you did here, nobody can ever take it from you."

"I thank you," I told him, unsure of why I was getting the attention.

"Don't bother with returning to your tank, Ha'almo'or," Most High A'armo'o said. "Emergency services has taken over, but it appears that you have rescued any and all who remained within the city."

"There has to be more," I said softly, staring to turn around to look at the burning city.

Most High A'armo'o touched my cheek, preventing me from turning.

"If there is, it is up to Emergency Services now," he said softly. "The Precursors have been forced from the system, destroyed here on the ground."

I just nodded.

"Now comes the hard part, loyal one," Most High A'armo'o said.

"What is that?" I asked.

He was silent for moment.

"Living with it," the Terran said.

His words echoed in my soul.

"There is still a war to fight, Ha'almo'or, and I wish you as part of my Herd," A'armo'o said, breaking the uncomfortable silence.

"Of course, Most High," I said.

"We're loading onto ships, joining the Terrans. There are multiple worlds under threat. Join us," Most High A'armo'o said.

"I will follow you wherever you go," I swore.

"Gather your faithful crew, Ha'almo'or," Most High A'armo'o said. "We will head for the Terran's recovery point at dawn."

"My crew are neo-sapients," I said and tensed, waiting for their rejection.

Most High A'armo'o gave an odd motion I had learned was a Terran shrug.

"If they are your crew, they are your crew," he said.

"Welcome to the Atomic Hooves," the big Terran said. He spit again and looked me in the eyes. "See you onboard the ships."

I looked at Most High A'armo'o. "We are leaving the Great Herd?"

He nodded. "I am. Others are joining me. Will you?"

I turned and looked at the city.

There were other worlds, other cities.

Others who will need me.

"I will, Most High."

Printed in Poland
by Amazon Fulfillment
Poland Sp. z o.o., Wrocław
03 April 2022

56580124-ecc9-444a-815a-042912f30f5dR01